A CHRISTMAS EMBRACE

"Christmas is next week," Augusta said. "The children think Clarissa is going to magically reappear with their wonderful Christmas surprise in tow. They honestly believe it, Richard. How am I going to deal with their disappointment?"

"How are *we* going to deal with it?" he said softly. "I am going to be with you and the children on Christmas, if you will be good enough to invite me."

"I think you are the kindest gentleman who ever lived," she said soulfully.

He noted her brandy glass was empty again. "That is enough for you," he said humorously as he placed the bottle beyond her reach.

Augusta laughed and stood up. She offered her hand.

"Thank you for humoring me. I will intrude upon your privacy no longer."

He looked at her proffered hand quizzically for a moment. Then he kissed her on the cheek. With a sigh of surrender, she leaned toward him and laid her head for a moment on his shoulder as he held her close. . . .

Books by Kate Huntington

THE CAPTAIN'S COURTSHIP

THE LIEUTENANT'S LADY

LADY DIANA'S DARLINGS

MISTLETOE MAYHEM

A ROGUE FOR CHRISTMAS

THE MERCHANT PRINCE

TOWN BRONZE

HIS LORDSHIP'S HOLIDAY SURPRISE

Published by Zebra Books

HIS LORDSHIP'S HOLIDAY SURPRISE

Kate Huntington

ZEBRA BOOKS
Kensington Publishing Corp.
http://www.kensingtonbooks.com

ZEBRA BOOKS are published by

Kensington Publishing Corp.
850 Third Avenue
New York, NY 10022

All Kensington titles, imprints and distributed lines are available at special quantity discounts for bulk purchases for sales promotion, premiums, fund-raising, educational or institutional use.

Special book excerpts or customized printings can also be created to fit specific needs. For details, write or phone the office of the Kensington Special Sales Manager: Kensington Publishing Corp., 850 Third Avenue, New York, NY 10022. Attn. Special Sales Department. Phone: 1-800-221-2647.

First Printing: October 2003
10 9 8 7 6 5 4 3 2 1

Printed in the United States of America

This book is dedicated with much affection to the memory of my grandparents Katie and William Saluke, in gratitude for a childhood full of magical Christmas Eves.

Prologue

Miss Augusta Oglethorpe's eyes narrowed as she watched her lovely widowed sister, Clarissa, smile up into the wicked dark eyes of the devastatingly handsome Richard, Marquess of Ardath. He wore his Scots heritage plainly in the high, aristocratic bridge of his nose and his bladelike cheekbones. His lean, powerful figure in evening dress made all the other men in the room look insignificant.

Not that Augusta was impressed by such superficial traits.

The marquess seemed to sense the power of her gaze and lifted his eyebrows at her.

With a sniff of distaste, she averted her eyes, but not before she saw him whisper something into Clarissa's ear. It caused Clarissa to look in Augusta's direction and laugh.

"I'd keep an eye on your sister, if I were you," Mrs. Bonner, their hostess, said gaily. "Lord Ardath's conquests are said to number in the hundreds, and that is only *this* season."

"I will keep it in mind," Augusta said, refusing to let Clarissa's flirtations and that unprincipled rake ruin her evening.

Like most of London, Mrs. Bonner and her husband

would flee for the country next week in preparation for Christmas and the New Year. Leading to the holiday itself would be a series of house parties and other country entertainments.

Augusta wished them joy of all their frivolous social discourse. In a few weeks, London would be thin of company, but that was when Augusta liked it best. She would attend lectures at the British Museum, meet friends at the circulating library, and spend the long winter evenings before the fire in the parlor of her small, neat house reading books and petting her cat.

Absolute heaven.

In addition to that, she would be engaged in preparations for the party she gave every year for the indigent gentlewomen of London. They so looked forward to it, as did she. Her house would be full of greenery, the table would be groaning with food, and every corner of the house would be filled with candlelight and excellent conversation, for all the single ladies of less modest means with whom Augusta socialized would attend as well.

Just a simple, civilized, enjoyable party for Augusta and like-minded females. The very best time of her year.

Augusta loved Christmas in London.

Richard, the Marquess of Ardath, hated Christmas in London, but going to his ancestral home in Scotland would be even worse.

There were too many ghosts there. His parents. His brother. All dead now.

All about him, these good people were making plans to go into the country, to their house parties and their noisy gatherings of friends and family. Richard turned down invitations to join them by the score. As usual, he would spend Christmas alone in his hunting box, shooting pheasant by day, drinking smuggled brandy and reading by the fire at night.

Strangely, the thought of this time that he normally welcomed as a period of quiet renewal seemed unspeakably lonely. He suddenly felt old, even though he was only thirty.

He looked down into Clarissa Fenshaw's lovely cornflower blue eyes and thought how appealing it would be to share the hunting box with the beautiful, sensual, accommodating widow. He had been seeing her socially for some months, ever since she came to London upon completion of her period of mourning for her late husband. She was cheerful, kind, and passionate. He touched her cheek with his gloved hand as he bent to whisper a suggestion into her ear.

When he did, he once again encountered the eye of Miss Augusta Oglethorpe, who was watching him with a look of utter disdain on her face.

The two sisters could not have been more unlike in temperament, although there was a superficial family resemblance between them. Both were tall, with elegant, willowy figures, and had masses of lovely dark curling hair. Clarissa's was dressed in artful curls around her perfect, heart-shaped face. The prim Miss Oglethorpe's was pulled back into an austere chignon.

Clarissa was a vision in celestial blue gauze; Miss Oglethorpe wore pearl gray muslin made up close to the throat.

A smile trembled on Clarissa's lush, sensual lips as she looked up into his eyes.

Miss Oglethorpe's expression suggested that she recently had eaten sour prunes.

Oh, how disapproving the prim spinster would look if she knew what plans the wicked marquess had for her pretty sister *this* holiday!

One

December 1813
The Marquess of Ardath's hunting box

Jilted.

Richard, the Marquess of Ardath, washed the bitter taste of the word from his mouth with a glass of the best French champagne, smuggled at exorbitant expense into England to please a faithless female who dared spurn his distinguished title, his enormous fortune, and, if a succession of infatuated ladies over the years were to be believed, his not inconsiderable powers of seduction.

The bitter taste was just as strong after four glasses of champagne as it had been before the first.

"Dinner is served, your lordship," his butler announced.

"Don't want it," Richard said, sighing. For once he cursed his hard head for liquor. He would have wished to be pleasantly sedated on such an occasion. Instead he was painfully sober. He had eaten nothing since breakfast, but he could not bear the filet of sole, the pâté de foie gras and succulent purple grapes, the asparagus with white sauce and truffles, the hothouse strawberries and fresh cream that he had ordered conveyed to this secluded place to please the woman he had been given every reason to think eagerly anticipated the consummation of their union.

Unfortunately, there was little else to eat in the house.

The scent of the hothouse roses that filled the little hunting box sickened him.

"You must eat something, my lord," ventured Minton, unintimidated by the black glare Richard cast him. The butler had come to Ardath in Richard's father's time and had known him from the time he was a child.

Unfortunately, in Richard's present state, a demonstration of sympathy was likely to unman him.

"Go away," Richard said through gritted teeth.

Minton compressed his lips in disapproval and obeyed.

Richard scowled at the half-filled glass of flat champagne in his hand and deliberately threw it across the room into the fireplace.

Minton poked his head back into the doorway, made a silent assessment of the situation, and withdrew, looking affronted.

Good, Richard thought with mean satisfaction. Maybe they would leave him alone now. He had imported his principal servants from his town house to ensure he and his bride received the most impeccable and discreet service possible during what was to be this magical prelude to their marriage. Now he wished he had left the concerned busybodies at home. With the slightest encouragement, he would have them all in here clucking over him.

At that moment, an urgent knocking sounded at the door.

Richard raised his eyebrows. Who would come calling at this hour of the night in such a secluded place?

Minton walked in his usual unhurried, dignified gait toward the summons and opened the door with all the majesty he employed when he presided over Richard's town house during the height of the season.

Richard gave a smile of sour satisfaction when he heard a woman's voice raised in mingled demand and entreaty.

So, he thought. *The fair Clarissa has come to her senses.*

Well, if she decided she wanted to be a marchioness after all—and evidently she did, or she would not have come here—she would have to beg.

Would he forgive her? That depended upon how persuasively she did so.

He thought of the carefully prepared bedchamber upstairs with distaste.

No.

Not even if she begged.

A man had to have *some* pride.

"Set the dogs on her," he shouted.

"Uncle Richard!" cried a small voice.

Well, he thought, taken aback, he *had* told Clarissa's children they could call him that.

How like an unprincipled woman to bring her children along to soften him up.

"Cynthia?" he said, going to one knee as a tiny blond girl dressed in a haphazardly buttoned blue velvet coat managed to get around the butler, who was blocking her way, and run forward to cast herself on Richard's bosom. The four-year-old was followed by Gerald, her three-year-old red-haired brother.

He forced himself to smile at the weary children. It was not *their* fault their mother was a traitoress. He rose and stood with a hand on each child's head as he waited for the bedraggled female to approach him. She was holding the youngest child, two-year-old, er, Harry, Richard believed the child's name was. In truth, Richard did not know the children well, although he had been determined to do his duty with regard to them, which he had not expected to be arduous. He had simply ordered the nurseries of his primary estate opened and refurbished to receive Clarissa's brood.

Ah. Mother and child, he thought sarcastically. A touching picture, carefully designed to soften his heart.

Only, instead of cuddling the boy to her breast and simpering at Richard, she was holding the child awkwardly, as if she didn't know quite what to do with his arms and legs. She looked about her and unceremoniously dumped the child into Minton's arms in such a way that he either had to accept the boy or allow him to fall to the ground.

"If you wake him up," she said with a gimlet stare at the butler, "I shall cut your heart out. He has been wailing these past two hours."

She turned on Richard with a look of pure fury on her face. He staggered back a few steps.

He had been misled by the dark hair, elegant cheekbones and tall, graceful figure—not to mention the trio of somewhat familiar children in her company—into mistaking this woman for Clarissa.

But instead of Clarissa's clear cornflower blue, this woman had eyes of dark brown, and they were looking daggers at him.

Augusta Oglethorpe.

Egad.

Just what he needed when his spirits were at low ebb—Clarissa's disapproving bluestocking of a sister, who had always looked at him as if he were a bug swimming in her tea.

He had never seen Miss Oglethorpe anything but self-possessed and meticulously turned out in her prim, well-cut clothes and with every dark hair tortured into obedience.

But now her hair was straggling from its pins, her hat was all askew, and her clothing was rumpled. Her nose was red, as if she had been crying, although Richard suspected it was just the cold. Her steps were halting, for obviously her limbs were stiffened from spending some time on the road, but there was nothing whatsoever wrong with her voice.

"Where is she, you unprincipled blackguard?" she demanded. She forgot herself so much as to grasp the lapels of his coat and give him a shake that almost caused her to topple over. Reflexively, he clasped her arm to steady her, and she drew back from his touch as if he were the devil incarnate.

"What the dev—" He glanced at the two older children's attentive faces and bit off the expletive he had been about to utter. "What are you doing here, Miss Oglethorpe?" he amended hastily.

"I have come to deliver my poor sister from your treacherous hands, as if you did not know," she spat out. "I went to your house and learned that you had come here."

Her gaze took in the room filled with Clarissa's favorite pink roses and the bucket of ice containing the empty bottle of champagne. She gave him a look that would cut glass.

"You *lecher!*" she cried as she pushed past him and went up the stairs, followed in haste by Richard. Minton had the presence of mind to block the two other children with his body when they would have followed them.

"See here," Richard said, embarrassed that Clarissa's sister should see the extravagant preparations he had made for the faithless minx. He strode in front of her and grasped her shoulders to halt her progress, but she stepped down hard on his stockinged foot.

"Miss Oglethorpe! You can't go in there!" he shouted as she quickly darted around him and into the bedchamber.

"Aha!" she cried. "I knew it!"

Richard gave a long sigh of humiliation. There were roses in this room, too, a fragrant symphony of red, pink, and yellow in crystal vases on every surface. There were white beeswax candles in crystal candelabra. The counterpane was pink satin, and the sheets were scented with rosewater.

"You filthy scoundrel," the woman said. She raised her voice. "Clarissa!" she shouted. "Come out! I know you are hiding in here. I have come to take you home."

"She is not here," Richard said. "Come away, now."

"Not on your life," she said. "Not until I've found my sister. Clarissa!"

As Richard watched, she went to the wardrobe and cast it open to find only his clothes there. She poked through them with her gloved hand as if she expected to find her sister cowering among them. She even dropped to her knees and looked under the bed.

He sighed and leaned against the fireplace mantel with his arms crossed.

After a moment, Miss Oglethorpe's shocked face peered over the counterpane at him.

"She is not here," she said in a choked voice. "She's really not here."

The sound of childish voices raised in argument reached them and, to Richard's consternation, the woman's shoulders began to shake as she drew herself upright. Abruptly, she sat down on the counterpane and let her head drop into her hands.

"What am I going to do?" she cried out in despair.

"See here," Richard said, appalled. The bloody female was falling apart, and he would be dashed if she was going to do it on the bloody satin counterpane he had purchased for her little tease of a sister. "Pull yourself together, woman!"

"I was certain she was here," she said, sniffling. "You and she have been somewhat discreet, but one would have to be blind not to know that eventually you would . . . do this!" She indicated the sumptuous furnishings with a distracted hand. "Villain! Lurking about, seducing perfectly respectable women—"

"Perfectly respectable! Clarissa?" he said, then had to add out of justice, "Well, *I* thought her respectable or I wouldn't have asked her to marry me. Little did I know she would serve me such a trick."

"Marry you?" Miss Oglethorpe repeated. "You intended to *marry* Clarissa? Do you think I am a *fool*, my lord?"

Goaded, he dug into the pocket of his coat until he found the rumpled special license signed personally by the Archbishop of Canterbury, no less.

"Good gracious," she said faintly when she had snatched and examined this article. Richard gave an unamused snort at the mild expletive.

Her eyes were huge with something akin to reverence as she stared at him.

"You were going to *marry* her," she said. Then she assaulted Richard's ears by giving a faint scream.

"What the deuce is the matter with you now?" he said with a sigh.

"She must be dead, or lying injured somewhere," she cried. She sprang at him and grasped the lapels of his coat again. "I was persuaded that she had given in to your blandishments to go off somewhere with you, but I never dreamed you intended to marry her. Something dreadful must have happened to her, for it is her chief ambition to marry well to provide for her children after poor Stephen's estate was found to be such a disappointment. You must send to Bow Street at once!"

He disengaged her surprisingly strong fingers from his person and put her away from him.

"Absolutely not," he said. "Your sister is nothing to me."

"But . . . but what am I to do with the children?" she asked, looking distraught. "She left them at my house while I was asleep two nights ago, then she went away without explanation. The letter she left for me said that the children's nurse had gone without notice, and she must go off into the country to think."

"Into the country to think? Clarissa?" he scoffed. "Without the shops or parties? With no one to flirt with except a few country squires? Highly unlikely."

"So I thought at the time," she admitted. "But the children—"

"Are none of my concern. I wash my hands of Clarissa, her children, and, I thank The Almighty, you. Leave my house, Miss Oglethorpe. Immediately, if you please."

She sank to the counterpane and began weeping.

"Stop that!" he said, disconcerted. "Stop that at once!"

She wept with great, wracking sobs, as if her heart would break. No coy play of long, wet eyelashes to get her own way, this, but a violent, gusty demonstration of utter despair that completely unmanned him.

"I cannot bear it," she said. "I know nothing about children. Two members of my staff have resigned. My poor cat is losing its hair. And from day to night there is this unbearable clattering in the house to the point where I am about to lose my mind."

"So you brought them here, into what you fully expected to be a scene of debauchery? Are you *insane?*"

"I did not know what else to do with them! It is easy for you. You are a *man!*"

"Easy," he sneered. "By God, that's rich!"

She blinked and looked around as if seeing the pink counterpane, the candles and the flowers with new eyes.

"Oh," she said in a small voice. "How inconsiderate of me. You must be . . . disappointed."

"Well, I did have plans for this evening other than entertaining Clarissa's disapproving watering pot of a sister and her children!"

"I must find her," Miss Oglethorpe said, pulling herself together.

She marched down the stairs with head held high and relieved the butler of the awake and cranky two-year-old.

"Come, children. We are leaving," she said.

At that, all three set up such a fit of wailing that Richard fought an impulse to cover his ears with his hands. His head was beginning to hurt.

"Can you not make them *stop?* How in . . . Hades can you tolerate that unceasing *noise?*" he asked.

"I can't," she admitted with a rueful sigh. "I think

my hair is going to fall out, too. Come along, Cynthia. Gerald. We must go back to London now."

"I want my mama!" cried Cynthia.

"I'm hungry!" cried Gerald.

"I'm sorry, my dears," Miss Oglethorpe said, looking tired. "Your mother is not here, after all, and Lord Ardath wants us to go away."

"Uncle Richard," said Cynthia, looking pathetic as a single tear rolled down from one melting cornflower blue eye.

Her mother's daughter, but blameless for Clarissa's sins.

Richard could not let them go like that. Not *hungry*.

"What have we in the kitchen that children can eat?" Richard asked Minton.

"Dinner *has* been served this past quarter hour, my lord," Minton said with superb dignity. "Will you and your guests go in?"

Richard raised his eyebrows at Miss Oglethorpe and extended his arm, for all the world like a good host. She gave a half-hysterical laugh and accepted with her free hand as Harry fussed against her shoulder. Cynthia trotted on ahead.

Gerald clutched Richard's leg as he escorted the odd little party into his dining room.

Two

Cynthia took a big bite of the pâté de foie gras that the Marquess of Ardath had procured at exorbitant expense and not inconsiderable trouble for the delectation of his future bride and spat it out on the spotless white damask tablecloth.

Gerald wrinkled his nose at the filet of sole covered in slivered almonds and proclaimed, "Don't like fish."

The children's reaction to the very rare roast sirloin that left a puddle of blood on the serving platter was equally unenthusiastic.

Augusta, after sampling the voluptuous richness of the pâté, started to pick up an oyster on the half shell and remembered in time what properties they were said to contain. She gave the marquess a sharp look of disapproval.

The man had the gall to laugh out loud, although the sound had a bit of hysteria to it.

He caught Minton's eye.

"Clear this away except for the bread and strawberries, and bring us something suitable for children," he said.

Minton looked perplexed.

"I am not certain what that would be, my lord," he said. "And I fear Pierre—"

"Quite right. Pierre is spewing Gallic expletives and threatening to swim back to France. Never mind, Minton. I shall take care of it. Watch the children. Miss Oglethorpe and I will return in a moment." He rose and extended his arm to Augusta.

Always the perfect gentleman, she thought sourly as she accepted it and left the room with him. Behind them came the unmistakable sound of china hitting the floor and shattering into a thousand pieces.

The marquess winced, but after a moment of hesitation he guided Augusta's steps forward. He caught her arm when she would have turned back.

"Minton will contrive to deal with the situation," he said. "You must forgive my staff. Mine is a bachelor household."

"So is mine," she said with a sigh. "An unmarried gentlewoman's household, to be more precise. There must be something here they can eat."

"I hope so," he said. "I somehow think a diet of bread and strawberries isn't the most salubrious one for children."

Augusta could have wept again, although she refused to disgrace herself further in front of this man. She had meant to be such a *good* aunt when the children were born. And, indeed, she was quite attached to them—in theory, at least. But she had seen little of her married sister and her children when Clarissa's husband was still alive because they lived in York, and Augusta stayed primarily in London except for a few weeks' holiday each summer in Bath. Until the children were abruptly dropped on her doorstep, her only obligations to them were letters with small gifts on their birthdays and the occasional visit to York while her poor sister was in mourning.

"I am a terrible aunt," she said. The realization was a bitter one. "I should have stopped sooner and procured something for them to eat, but I was so determined to reach my sister tonight."

"We shall contrive something," he said.

He must think her the greatest ninnyhammer who ever lived. She, who prided herself on her intelligence and common sense.

The chef, she saw at a glance, was not happy. He scowled at the two of them when they had the gall to invade his kitchen.

The marquess gave him a cool nod and went straight to the pantry. He emerged with a small container of oats and handed it to the chef.

"Porridge takes *forever*," Augusta said. "We don't have that long."

"In the meantime we have fruit and bread. And cheese."

Incredibly, Augusta gave an involuntary laugh. Who would have thought she was capable of it?

"Cynthia says all of your cheese stinks."

The chef burst into a tirade of impassioned French at this sacrilege. The Roquefort and Stilton cheeses had, like the pâté de foie gras, been procured at great expense to please the palates of a pair of sophisticated lovers.

"Yes, yes. I know, Pierre," the marquess said in English. He knew the chef could understand him perfectly well. "They are, indeed, ignorant savages, but there is nothing I can do about that now. Shall we try them with the champagne?"

Augusta gave him such a shocked look that he sighed.

"Merely jesting," he said, "although it might put them to sleep."

An hour later, when Minton bore the porridge into the dining room, all three children were still awake and cranky. Augusta was in despair at the thought of putting the poor little things back into the carriage to repair to the nearest inn, which was probably many miles away.

How could she have dragged them all this way for nothing?

Cynthia took a monogrammed silver spoon and poked it into the porridge.

"It has *things* in it," she complained.

"Apples and walnuts. And cinnamon," the marquess said. "You will like it." To Augusta, he added, "Pierre is incapable of cooking ordinary food. He simply can't bring himself not to embellish the simplest thing."

Augusta had noticed this. Even the cream served with the strawberries had vanilla and sugar whipped into it.

The marquess smiled into Cynthia's mutinous face and dipped a clean spoon into her porridge to taste it.

"Delicious," he said, smiling.

Cynthia watched him a moment, then tried some of her own. Gerald, who had been watching the marquess intently, ate some, too.

Harry, bless the child, had crawled into Augusta's lap without complaint and was eating the porridge she fed to him with every appearance of pleasure.

"Teeth!" she cried out at once. "Does a child this age have all his teeth? He will not choke on the apples and walnuts, will he?"

"I haven't the faintest idea," the marquess admitted. He rushed to her side, went down on one knee, and pried Harry's mouth open. The child grinned and allowed the porridge to slide from his jaws. Reflexively, the marquess caught the mess in his hand, then he looked at it as if he could not quite believe what he was seeing.

"He has teeth," the marquess said dryly as he reached for a serviette. "At least he doesn't bite."

When he returned to his place at the table, he was surprised when Cynthia walked over to him and put one soft, dimpled hand on his knee.

"I want to sit on your lap," she said.

Her mother's daughter, indeed, thought Richard, but he had to smile. Despite her imperious ways, the little girl was a charmer. He lifted her up and reached for her porridge to place it in front of her. Perfectly content, she ate the rest of the porridge without complaint.

Soon Richard felt a tug on his coat and peered down into Gerald's earnest face.

"Mama forgot to bring the soldier to Aunt 'Gusta's house," he said, laying his head on Richard's knee. "I miss him."

The toy soldier. A casual gift he had brought to Clarissa's rented house as an afterthought the day he met her children. It touched him that the child valued it.

"I am sorry, Gerald," he said. "Perhaps we can fetch it from your mama's house."

"No," the boy said sadly. "Mama went away. The landlord does not know where she is gone. Aunt 'Gusta said there is no one living in the house now. Maybe Mama left the soldier all alone in a strange place, like she did us."

A strange place.

Richard stole a glance at Miss Oglethorpe to see how she was taking this.

Not well.

"Why did I not think to bring along some of the toys Clarissa left at my house with the children?" she said. "The soldier was not with them. Gerald has been asking for it since he arrived."

The woman did care for them, Richard realized. She simply did not know *how* to care for children.

Well, that made two of them.

Gerald walked to the window and looked outside.

"Snow!" he said happily.

Cynthia, not to be left out, went to join him at the window.

"That is nice, dear," Augusta said absently. Then she sat up so abruptly that Harry opened one eye to peer up at her, then closed it and lapsed back to sleep.

"Snow!" she cried, and carried the sleeping child to the window. When she looked at Richard, her eyes were wild. "We must leave here at once!"

"Whatever are you talking about?" Richard said.

"If I stay the night, I shall be compromised."

"Of all the silly . . ."

Bloody hell. She was *right.*

"Come, children. Put on your coats," she said. "We must go."

Richard nodded to a footman, who left for the stables to ready the lady's horses and carriage for the journey.

Cynthia's little fists knotted, and her arms were so stiff that no matter how hard Augusta struggled, she could not get her coat on her.

"I don't want to go with you," the child cried. She

smiled beatifically into Richard's face. "I want to go with *him.*"

"Me, too!" cried Gerald. "I want to go with Uncle Richard."

"But Uncle Richard is not going back to town, Gerald." She clutched the youngest child to her and looked as if she might weep again.

Anything but that.

Richard had expected to stay ensconced in the hunting box with his bride until the New Year. Now, looking around at the love nest he had created for his bride, he wondered what could have possessed him to turn his favorite manly retreat into this temple to feminine vanity.

He hated London this time of the year. But he hated more the thought of languishing here a moment longer in his hurt pride and disappointment. The place would never be the same for him.

Sulking. That's what he had been doing here. Sulking.

How pathetic.

"Minton! I am for London. Send someone to have my traveling coach readied."

"But, my lord! On such a night?" Minton blurted out. Then he looked down in shame at having forgotten himself and his position to such an extent.

"If the lady can travel, so can I. But separately, of course." Richard nodded to Miss Oglethorpe, whose mouth was hanging open. "We must not compromise the lady's precious reputation."

"I want to go with you, Uncle Richard," Cynthia declared again.

"Me, too," said Gerald.

"Thank heaven Harry is asleep," Miss Oglethorpe

said, giving in to self-pity, "or he would want to go with you, too."

"We *could* go in the same carriage, you know," he suggested. "My traveling coach is quite large and comfortable."

She looked absolutely appalled.

"Ride through the night with *you*, my lord?" she exclaimed. "Certainly not!"

"You flatter yourself, madam," he said stiffly as he bent to pick up Cynthia and Gerald and stood with one in either arm. He turned to his butler with a sigh.

"You may as well help Pierre pack up the food, close up the house, and accompany the rest of the servants back to the town house in London tomorrow. I do not suppose Miss Oglethorpe will permit me to return here until I discover what has become of her wretched sister."

"Thank you, my lord," Miss Oglethorpe said.

He merely scowled at her.

This was the deuce of a way to spend what he had expected to be his wedding night.

Three

Augusta stayed alone at the second inn she came to in her mad flight from Lord Ardath's hunting box. At the first, she was permitted to change horses, but the innkeeper's wife insisted that she ran a respectable house and no single lady with a child and no sign of a male escort or maid was going to spend the night under her roof!

Everyone knew that only one kind of female—and the innkeeper's wife didn't consider any such person a lady—traveled alone and with no baggage. Apparently poor exhausted little Harry didn't count.

Therefore, Augusta spent a virtually sleepless night at the second inn, which apparently had more relaxed standards. She tried in vain to quiet Harry, who was screaming with temper because he wanted to pet the pretty horses in the stable instead of going inside to bed. She felt covered in shame as she carried the red-faced child into the inn. To her consternation, the men loitering outside ogled her so thoroughly that she rushed straight to her room to bar the door.

Harry quickly succumbed to the sleep of the just and the young, and snored all night. Not that Augusta could have slept, anyway. The snow on the road had been quite deep. She would never forgive herself if

Gerald, Cynthia, and the marquess came to harm. It would be all her fault for insisting upon traveling to London this night.

Her precious reputation did not seem so important now.

When she finally arrived at her town house, it was to find her staff engaged in thorough housecleaning in preparation for Augusta's annual Christmas party, and her once luxuriantly fluffy ginger cat hiding under her bed. It took her quite a quarter of an hour to coax it out, and when it saw Harry, it darted back into hiding again.

The memory of the demon children who had appeared unexpectedly one night apparently lingered. Augusta's housekeeper said the cat ran for this refuge every time the front door was opened, and Augusta didn't blame it in the least.

"Send to the Marquess of Ardath's town house to inquire whether his staff has received word of his lordship and the children," Augusta told her housekeeper.

"Yes, miss," the housekeeper said.

"And find something for Master Harry to eat."

"Not hungry," said Harry.

"Or see if one of the footmen will watch him for a little while so I can sleep."

"Want to go with you," said Harry, clinging to Augusta's skirts.

"Come along, then," she said in resignation as she smoothed Harry's baby-fine brown hair. "Let us lie down for a short sleep."

"Not sleepy," said the child.

"Then come along to keep me company," Augusta suggested. "But you must be very, very quiet so I can sleep."

"Yes, Aunt 'Gusta," he said.

He was true to his word, but as Augusta dozed on her bed she could hear him going through the contents of her dressing table, presumably to find something he could play with. It was like listening to rodents chewing on the wainscoting.

"Not the French scent!" she cried when she opened one eye to see what the suddenly quiet Harry was doing. Her heart nearly stopped when she saw he had the delicate glass bottle in his small, chubby, perpetually moist hands.

He was so startled he nearly dropped it.

"That's a good boy," she said in the most soothing voice she could muster. "Put it on the table now."

He did so, and turned to her with his lower lip trembling.

"Mama lets us play with the pretty bottles," he said as tears filled his eyes.

"Oh, Harry," Augusta said.

The little boy walked across the room and lifted his arms so she could pull him into bed with her. He cuddled close to her and she stroked his hair.

"I miss Mama," he said on a watery hiccup.

"I know you do, dear," Augusta said, feeling like an ogre.

His nose was running and Augusta absentmindedly swept it with her hand, then looked about for something to wipe the slimy substance on. She stared at her hand with distaste and spied a linen handkerchief on her bedside table, which she put to use.

Poor lost little boy.

Where on earth *was* his mother?

* * *

Augusta raised herself up on one elbow when the housekeeper came to the door of her bedchamber. She really must see about hiring a lady's maid, or she would lose Mrs. Creely, too. It was not fair for her to be expected to act as personal maid and housekeeper both. Her maid had spent two days in the household with the children and, nerves shattered, given her resignation without notice on the spot. When Augusta pointed out to the shuddering maid that she would have great difficulty finding another position without a reference from her last employer, she merely fled from her presence to pack her bag and leave.

Indeed, Augusta had felt more envy than anger at her desertion. She had lost an upstairs maid as well.

"Yes?" she said with an encouraging nod to the housekeeper.

"The Marquess of Ardath to see you, miss, with Mr. Gerald and Miss Cynthia."

"I'll come down," Augusta said. She touched Harry's shoulder and he roused.

"Gerald and Cynthia are here," she said.

"Want to go home to Mama," he whined.

"How I wish you could," Augusta muttered, and went to the mirror to tidy her hair, which looked as if she had been pulled through a hedge backward. Her clothes were rumpled, too, but they would have to do.

She took Harry's hand and went down to the parlor, expecting to find the marquess wild-eyed and ready to run crazed into the street. She almost smiled at the prospect of seeing the marquess as tired and rumpled as she was.

Instead, every dark hair on his handsome head was in place and his expertly tailored clothes bore not a crease. His dark eyes were clear and alert. When he caught sight of her, he had the gall to look amused.

Gerald walked right over to his little brother and gave him a shove, which caused Harry to fall onto his plump bottom and start to cry. When Gerald bent over him, Harry pulled his brother's leg out from under him so they were *both* sitting on the floor and wailing.

Augusta picked up Harry, and the marquess picked up Gerald.

Just like him, Augusta thought resentfully, to pick up the child whose nose was not running. Harry buried his face in Augusta's bosom and left a streak of mucus on the front of her gown, but she was beyond all caring.

"Uncle Richard has beautiful horses," Cynthia said, eyes shining. "He let us take turns riding with the coachman."

"In the middle of winter?" Augusta said in horror.

"Only for a quarter hour at a time," said the marquess, "and they were warmly wrapped in blankets, I assure you."

Augusta suspected he'd merely wanted to get them out of the carriage for a little while, but she let this pass. In truth, she wished she had thought of this on the way to his hunting box, when the children were driving her demented with their bickering.

"You seem to be quite the authority on children," she said resentfully.

"I was one once," he said. "I have my doubts about you."

"Whatever can you mean?"

"One would suspect you had no memory at all of what it is to be a child."

"I am not accustomed to children. I told you this."

"They are people, like any other," the marquess said with a shrug. "It is a good thing I have my old nurse installed at my town house."

"A nurse," Augusta exclaimed. "You have a nurse?"

"Why are you so surprised? You know very well I expected to marry your sister."

"Yes, of course," she said. "Do you think your nurse would be interested in coming to work for me?"

"Highly unlikely. She was looking forward to dandling my children on her knee. She still is, despite the way things turned out. She certainly has more optimism than I."

Augusta instantly forgave him his rested eyes, spotless appearance, and superior tone.

"How could I have forgotten your great disappointment?" she asked.

"Well, yes," he said, looking down at his hands.

"At the risk of being presumptuous, I can only assure you that someday you will love again."

"My good girl, are you imagining my heart broken?" he said, looking up with sardonic laughter in his eyes. "I could love again, as you so quaintly put it, this very night, if I wished. I have only to send a message to one of several ladies of my acquaintance—"

"Lord Ardath! The children!" Augusta cried. She clapped her hands over Harry's ears, and he looked up at her with a question in his innocent eyes.

"Well, *you* are the one who introduced the subject."

"I was speaking of my sister, not one of your . . ." She made a finicky little gesture with one hand that made Richard laugh out loud.

"All that would have been at an end when I married Clarissa," he said. He gave her a rueful look. "Or almost at an end. I intended to reform my wicked ways, I assure you."

"You *were* in love with her."

Richard could not bear the pity on the woman's face.

"I am surprised to hear such mawkish sentimentality from the lips of a lady who so prides herself on her intelligence. I was *never* in love with Clarissa Fenshaw," he declared. "Love is the invention of fools and poets. But your sister is a beautiful and, I thought, complaisant woman who had the sophistication not to expect me to live in her pocket once we were married. She had already demonstrated her ability to breed sons, and this is important to a man with a centuries-old title and vast estates. Clarissa knew my reasons for seeking the match, and she agreed that we would suit."

"Such a romantic proposal," Miss Oglethorpe said dryly. "How astounding that she did not find such a prospect irresistible."

"I paid her the very great compliment of being honest with her. Your sister, my dear Miss Oglethorpe, could have given lessons to a merchant in extracting the highest payment for her goods."

"How dare you describe Clarissa in such terms!"

"I meant no criticism," he said, pleased to see the fire of temper in her dark eyes. It improved her countenance immensely. "I went to a great deal of trouble to please your sister, and I would have gone to more."

He looked down at Cynthia, who was sitting by his feet picking at the fringe of an embroidered pillow that she had pulled down from the sofa. Little wisps of fuzz from the fringe clung to the blue velvet coat his old nurse had brushed so carefully that morning.

"Her children," he said softly, "would have been my children."

"I did not know," she said. "I did not suspect . . ."

Richard knew he had said too much. No, he had not been in love with Clarissa. That was for unfledged boys. But it was well past time for him to marry, and he had expected loyalty, at least, from the lady he had chosen to bear his name.

The pity was back in Miss Oglethorpe's eyes. Dash it!

"Happily, your sister did me the very great favor of revealing her true nature before my ring was on her finger."

"I cannot understand how she could have served you such a turn," she said. "Unless something had happened to prevent her from meeting you."

"We are back to that again, are we?" he scoffed. "I have alerted Bow Street and hired runners to discover her whereabouts."

"Thank you, my lord," Miss Oglethorpe said. "I pray she will be found safe." She glanced anxiously at the children.

"I am sure you do. Else they will be left on your hands forever."

"If they are, I shall do my best for them," she said hotly. "What kind of a person do you think I am?"

"One seriously out of her depth," he replied, and she gave a gusty sigh of agreement.

"I will have to cancel my party," she said sadly. "The ladies will be *so* disappointed. But my duty to my sister's children must come first. And if the runners return with tragic news . . ." She could not go on.

"They won't," he said bracingly. "The woman jilted me and ran off with another man. Or she went somewhere to hide. She appears to have many friends. In fact, I know she was invited to some house party over Christmas, and I have sent one of the runners to see if she has gone there to elude me."

"You will not . . . do anything to her, will you? She is a *mother*, after all."

Richard laughed again.

"You, my proper Miss Oglethorpe, have been reading too many lurid novels," he said with mock sternness. "Who would have suspected?"

"Nonsense," she said, coloring.

"Clarissa's precious person is safe from me. Indeed, I would be very happy never to see the woman again."

"Understandable," she said. She took a deep breath. "Did you bring the rest of the children's things? I am afraid I rushed off from the country without them."

"Yes. As I recall, you were in a blind panic to avoid having your reputation besmirched and being forced to marry me."

"Your mockery is uncalled for, my lord," she said with great dignity. "I am well aware that I would be no acceptable substitute for Clarissa. All the more reason to make sure my reputation remained intact."

"Such logic is irrefutable, madam," he said, standing. Cynthia raised her arms in silent appeal for him to pick her up.

"You must stay here, now, Cynthia," Miss Oglethorpe said, but clearly she was not happy about it.

"Don't want to stay with her," Gerald said, running to stand next to Richard.

Miss Oglethorpe looked insulted.

Richard looked from one pleading face to another. Out of Christian charity, he picked up Gerald and Cynthia.

At that moment, Miss Oglethorpe's cat gave a

bloodcurdling scream as Harry, who had been suspiciously quiet until now, pulled it out by the tail from under the sofa, where it had been hiding.

"Harry, *no!*" cried Miss Oglethorpe, rushing to rescue her cat where Harry had flung it. She tried to pick it up, but it hissed at her and streaked back under the sofa, leaving the bloody track of its claws on the back of her hand.

"My own cat *scratched* me," she said in hurt disbelief.

"Come along, Harry," Richard said hastily to the child, who was kneeling on the floor in front of the sofa, trying to reach the cat again. "You can all go home with me."

"My lord, this is unnecessary," Miss Oglethorpe said, but she could not prevent the look of relief that spread over her face.

"I know," he said. "But I have a nurse at my house, and you do not." He smiled at her. "Live to fight another day," he said. "You look weary, Miss Oglethorpe. Recruit your strength while you can. You are going to need it."

"Too true," she said ruefully. "Children, go with his lordship now." To Richard's surprise, she reached out to clutch his arm so he would look at her. "I would be grateful for a few hours of rest," she said, "but you must bring them back to me later this afternoon."

She actually seemed anxious that he do so.

"If something has happened to Clarissa," she said softly so the children would not hear, "they will be all of my family I have left."

"I will bring them," he promised.

Four

When the Marquess of Ardath returned to Miss Oglethorpe's house that afternoon, he was shown into her small library to find her writing at the table.

"My apologies for interrupting you," he said as he regarded the small stack of neatly folded papers in front of her. "Your butler did not tell me that you were engaged."

"I am happy to be interrupted from such a sad task," she said, looking up with her dark brown eyes just as weary as they had been when he left her that morning. "I am penning my regrets to all the ladies I invited to my Christmas party. It was to have been in four days."

"You did not rest at all, did you?" he said.

"No." She folded her hands in her lap. "I could not, with so much to do before the children were returned to me. I went to the registry office to see if I could hire a nurse and a nursemaid, but at Christmastime, it seems, there are few women seeking employment. They have all gone to be with their families and will not return until after the New Year."

"I am sorry," he said.

"So am I," she said with a tremulous smile. "And, of course, I could not delay in this task." She picked up one of the letters. "Although how I am to finish them all with the children in the house, I have no idea."

"There were a great many ladies invited to your party, then."

"Four-and-thirty. What a bleak Christmas it will be for them now."

"Will it? I am not much in the habit of celebrating Christmas. I usually go to my hunting box and spend the holiday alone. It is . . . peaceful there. I prefer it so."

His eyes dared her to contradict him.

"My cook roasts a goose," Miss Oglethorpe said, "and I have a few of my lady friends in, the ones who are alone. We have a fire in the parlor and discuss books. Sometimes we read to one another."

She gave a gusty sigh.

"It is so different from the Christmases of my childhood when my parents were alive. I know many fashionable persons do not observe the holiday except as an excuse to exchange visits and attend house parties, but my parents would invite all of our friends in the neighborhood to come to our house. We would have wagon rides around the yard, and Cook would spend days baking biscuits and apple tarts. We would skate on the pond. And on Christmas Eve my father and my uncles would bring in the Yule log."

"Yet you spend Christmas alone in London now."

"They are all gone now except for Clarissa, and she and her late husband lived in York. Neither had a taste for the country," she said. "It is going to be so difficult for the children if she does not come back before Christmas."

She pulled herself together with an effort.

"But none of this is your concern, my lord," she said. "I thank you for your assistance, and I regret the very great disappointment you have suffered at my sister's hands."

It was a dismissal.

He should be delighted to put the whole distasteful incident behind him, yet he could not accept. Never in his life had he left a lady in distress if he could help it, and he would not start now. Then there was the matter of Clarissa's children, whom he had promised his faithless prospective bride to treasure as his own. He had become rather accustomed to the idea.

"I will keep them until your party is over," he said, surprising them both. "It is only four days, after all."

Her mouth dropped open.

"This party seems to mean a great deal to you," he added.

"Yes," she said. "It does."

She stood and approached him with so much gratitude in her beautiful, tired eyes that for a moment he feared that she intended to cast herself upon his chest.

To prevent her from doing so, he said hastily, "But after that, they are yours."

"Of course," she said. "Once the party is over, you need not see any of us again."

"So we understand one another."

"My cat ran away," she blurted out.

"Your cat," he repeated blankly.

"One of the maids opened the door, and it ran right past her and out into the street. I probably will never see him again. I know it seems a small matter after all that has happened but . . ." Her voice cracked on the last word, and she could not seem to go on.

"I am very sorry," he said. "Truly." Cats were as children to spinsters, he knew. "Maybe he will come back."

She smiled wanly.

"If he did, I would have to make a choice between him and the children, and I must choose the children, of course. I had planned to ask a friend to take him, anyway, if Clarissa did not return."

She did not say what he was beginning to suspect himself.

Clarissa had stayed away too long. For all her frivolity, she *had* seemed a devoted mother. Perhaps something terrible *did* happen to her.

Richard grasped Miss Oglethorpe's hands in sympathy. They were cold, and he held them in his a moment to warm them.

"It will be all right," he said bracingly. "You have to be strong. For the children." He smiled. "And for the indigent ladies of London."

"Yes," she said. "I thank you, my lord."

"That's settled, then," he said. "Now that you no longer have to write all these letters of regret, we had best repair to your parlor. I brought Mrs. Kirby with me to help keep the children in order, but she is not as young as she was when I was a child."

Mrs. Kirby, Augusta found, was a stout, neatly dressed, sweet-faced woman of some sixty years who had the children lined up on the sofa and playing with their toys. Gerald and Harry each had a knight on horseback and were clanging them together. Cynthia had a doll with hair as golden and eyes as blue as her own.

They looked like little angels. Their hair was combed. Their clothes were pressed. Their faces were clean.

They never looked or behaved like this when they were with *her*.

"Uncle Richard said if we are very good, you will give us biscuits to eat," Cynthia said.

"And indeed I shall," Augusta said, glad that her cook had been baking this past week in anticipation of her party.

She pulled the bell and gave the order, and soon a maid came in carrying a tea tray. Behind her came another, carrying a pitcher of milk.

"Tea, my lord?" said Augusta, preparing to pour. It was good to be doing something with her old competence.

"Please," he said. He glanced over to where Mrs. Kirby was pouring milk for the children.

"She is a jewel," Augusta said. "Are you certain she would not care to work for me?"

"Perfectly certain," the marquess said.

We shall see, Augusta thought as she wondered how she might contrive to speak with Mrs. Kirby out of the marquess's hearing. Perhaps she could come to work for her temporarily, just until she found another nurse.

Or perhaps, after all, Clarissa would return just before Christmas, and Augusta could go back to her old comfortable, solitary life. Even after so short a time with the children, that serene other Augusta seemed a dream creature.

"Aunt 'Gusta," said Harry as he buried his face in her lap and left a milky trail of biscuit crumbs on her crisp, dark blue muslin gown. A mere week ago, she would have jumped up at once to change her gown lest a chance acquaintance unexpectedly pay a call and find her less than tidy, but the marquess had already seen her at her worst.

How far she had sunk below her former standards!

"What is it, my dear?" she asked Harry as he held his arms out to her and she caressed his wispy hair. At least *one* of Clarissa's children liked her. Indeed, she would never have admitted this to Clarissa, but Harry, the youngest, always had been her favorite.

"Want Mama," he said as she picked him up.

"I know, sweetheart," she whispered as she kissed his baby-warm cheek. "I do, too."

"Mama will be home for Christmas," Gerald said confidently. "Uncle Richard said we would have a big party at his house for all the neighborhood."

"Um, that was before, you know," Richard said, embarrassed, when Miss Oglethorpe gave him an incredulous look. He had made Clarissa's children many extravagant promises in anticipation of their marriage. He should have known that one of them would remember this particularly reckless vow.

"Uncle Richard said he would teach us how to skate," Cynthia said wistfully.

Good gad, he thought. *Whatever possessed me? I have not skated in years.*

"I am afraid . . . Uncle Richard has other commitments now," Miss Oglethorpe said. She looked as uncomfortable as Richard felt.

"He does not want us anymore," Cynthia said in a matter-of-fact voice that made Richard feel like a heartless cad, "because he is not going to marry Mama, after all."

"Why did Mama run away, Aunt 'Gusta?" asked Gerald plaintively.

"Mama will be back," Cynthia said with absolute conviction. "She would not leave us with *her* for Christmas. She said Aunt 'Gusta is a dried-up old maid."

On this pronouncement, Richard thought it wise to take his leave of Miss Oglethorpe and whisk the children away.

Her conscience would not permit her to abandon them to him completely, however.

"My servants and I will be bringing in the green tomorrow in anticipation of the party," she told him. "I should like you and the children to participate. Or, if you have other matters you must attend to, you could have Mrs. Kirby or one of your footmen escort them here."

"I do not understand," he said blankly.

"It is a country custom. We go outdoors and bring pine branches and holly and mistletoe into the house. Since I live in town, I send a pair of men out to the outskirts of the city to bring the green here. They put it on the doorstep, and the maids and I make decorations from it. I rather look forward to it, actually. I thought perhaps the children would like to help."

He hesitated.

She lowered her voice so the children would not hear. "It is most kind of you to offer to take care of them these next few days, but I do not wish to be a complete stranger to my sister's children."

"I will come," he said.

Gerald, Cynthia, and Harry had a lovely time trailing pine needles through their aunt's house and tying ribbons crookedly on the polished railings of the stairs. They ate quite as many biscuits, walnuts, and oranges as they tied into the kissing bough that the marquess, with the aid of a stout footman, attached to the chandelier in the parlor before he raised it again.

Richard gazed at the mistletoe and felt Miss Oglethorpe's eyes upon him. Did she know he had been thinking of Clarissa and of the very different way in which he had expected to spend this holiday?

It was customary for a gentleman to give a lady a chaste peck on the cheek when he found her lurking near the mistletoe, but Richard knew Miss Oglethorpe would consider such an action a gross impertinence.

If the children were not present, he would be tempted to do it, just to see her reaction. God knew he deserved a bit of entertainment. He had not been to his club once since his return to London, nor had he sent word to summon any of the less-than-strictly-respectable ladies of his acquaintance who would be pleased to help him find consolation for the desertion of the faithless Clarissa.

Instead, he found himself spending more and more time in his own nursery, attempting to distract Clarissa's children from their mother's continued absence.

It would be just a little kiss. What could it hurt?

He put his hands on Miss Oglethorpe's shoulders. Her eyes went huge in her startled face.

"My lord, I—" she began.

"Spit it out! Spit it out right now, Master Harry!" cried Mrs. Kirby, who had seized Harry and turned him upside down with a strength surprising in so elderly a lady.

"What is it?" said Richard, rushing at once to her side to grasp Harry when Mrs. Kirby's grip faltered.

"He swallowed some of those red berries," she said, looking distraught. "I fear they may be poisonous."

"Holly berries!" Augusta exclaimed. She snatched the child from Richard's arms and went right down on the floor with him. She held his face between her two hands. "Please, darling. Spit them out."

She put her finger in his mouth. He bit it. It was plain that he had already swallowed the berries.

Augusta took a deep breath. What was wanted now was resolution. As Harry bucked and whimpered, she stuck her finger down his throat and gave an almost savage cry of triumph when he vomited into her waiting hand, and she caught the excess in the skirt of her gown.

"There, darling," she said soothingly as she patted the child's back with her clean hand. "Mrs. Kirby, would you—"

"At once, miss," the nurse said as she took a serviette and wiped Augusta's hand and gown. She looked impressed. "You do that as if you had the experience of a dozen children under your care, miss, if you will permit my saying so."

"Thank you," Augusta said, taking the compliment in the spirit in which it was meant. "I have had to do so a number of times with my cat, for he has a habit of eating unwholesome objects, only I have to use a pencil because his throat is so narrow."

Harry, by this time, was weeping softly on Augusta's shoulder.

"There, there, love," she said soothingly. Her heart was racing. She could have *lost* him. So quickly, she could have lost him. "I am sorry we frightened you, Harry, but you must not put such things in your mouth."

The marquess was staring at her, looking dumbfounded. He whispered something to Mrs. Kirby, who pulled the bell and asked the maid to bring tea, a pitcher of milk, and a plate of biscuits to the parlor. Then she walked off with the maid to dispose of the soiled serviette.

Harry got up and toddled off on his sturdy little legs to join his brother and sister.

Augusta's knees were still shaking.

The marquess took her arm and assisted her to her feet.

"You were superb," he said in a voice filled with wonder, and kissed her full on the mouth.

Five

Richard reveled in the pleasurable exploration of soft, lush, pliant lips beneath his.

Then he came abruptly to his senses.

Egad! He was kissing Miss Oglethorpe.

He drew back and kept his eyes closed for a moment. In truth, he was afraid of what he might see when he opened them.

When he did open his eyes, he was somewhat relieved to see that Miss Oglethorpe looked just as appalled as he felt. The children, of course, were watching them with curious expressions on their faces. No doubt they would be full of questions later that he would be hard-pressed to answer.

Mrs. Kirby was trying valiantly to usher them from the room, presumably to prevent their witnessing any renewed depravity on his part.

Whatever *had* possessed him?

To his surprise, Miss Oglethorpe raised one well-shaped brow and answered his unspoken question.

"The mere euphoria of the moment, I presume," she said.

"Oh, absolutely. The most chaste kiss I have given any female since my adolescence, I assure you, Miss Oglethorpe," he said, striving for a careless tone.

"So I assume," she said, striving equally as hard to convey the impression that she had received infinitely more ardent kisses from gentlemen every day of the week and found his wanting. "I think, since you have already taken the greater liberty, that we may dispense with Miss Oglethorpe in favor of Augusta."

"Thank you," he said. "I find Miss Oglethorpe quite the mouthful, although Augusta, in its own way, is quite as daunting."

"You could call me 'Gusta, as the children do. Or even Gussie, as Clarissa did when she was a child."

"Absolutely not," he said. "Gussie sounds like the name of a milk cow. I could never call you that . . . Augusta."

Irrationally, her name, which she had always disliked, sounded almost like music when pronounced in his compelling baritone voice. She practically trembled with pleasure.

Stop that at once, she told her traitorous body.

"I appreciate that . . . Richard." She casually stepped back so she would be out from under the mistletoe.

He looked up and laughed, but he followed her example to give the deceptively harmless-looking sprig of green and white an equally wide berth.

"Mrs. Kirby," he called out. "It is safe to bring the children back into the room now."

The nurse poked her head through the doorway to ascertain for herself that Lord Ardath and Miss Oglethorpe were, indeed, behaving themselves. She ushered the children back into the room.

"Who would like a piece of orange?" asked the marquess as he seated himself comfortably on the sofa before a small serving table and selected a round, succulent fruit. He picked up a fruit knife and held it expectantly over the orange.

"I would," said Cynthia eagerly.

"Me," shouted Gerald.

"Me," echoed Harry.

"Ladies first, gentlemen," the marquess said, smiling.

She must think of him as *Richard* now, Augusta reminded herself. Naturally the marquess bore the Christian name of England's greatest medieval warrior-king, while hers conjured a mental vision of a many chinned Roman matron with a majestic beak of a nose.

Cynthia clapped her hands when Richard had deftly removed the peel and held a section of orange out to her. She bit into it and licked the juice from her lower lip with a fastidious, yet coy, flick of her tiny pink tongue that reminded Augusta painfully of her sister.

"Now yours, Augusta," he said, handing her a slice. His eyes were smiling as she bit into the sweet, succulent, sensual fruit, as if he knew that as a rule she rarely indulged in such luxuries as this. He had brought the oranges and the walnuts. If he had not, they would have decorated the kissing boughs with dried apples instead.

If Clarissa had married him as planned, she could have had oranges and walnuts—and champagne, pâté de foie gras, and ripe strawberries, for that matter—every day of her life, if she wished.

"Are you going to marry Aunt 'Gusta, Uncle Richard?"

Predictably, Cynthia was the first one to find her tongue. Augusta knew the children were not likely to be distracted by the oranges, delightful as they were, for long.

"No," he replied.

No.

Augusta's mind had been puzzling on how to answer this inevitable question since the moment Richard drew his lips from hers, leaving her senses tingling.

Sometimes when adults kiss, it doesn't mean anything, she might have said.

Or, *Uncle Richard merely wanted to thank Aunt Augusta for saving Harry's life.*

Or even, *Aunt Augusta has no intention of marrying any man. She is perfectly content with her small house and her circle of lady friends.*

No, he had said.

Baldly.

Unequivocally.

But at least he had the consideration not to shudder when he said it. That was something, she supposed.

Harry, bless him, chose that moment to provide a distraction from her disordered thoughts by climbing into her lap and giving her a messy, juice-flavored baby kiss on the lips.

Her heart melted when his chubby little arms went around her neck.

"I love you, Aunt 'Gusta," he said.

"I love you, too, Harry," she whispered. She hugged him again, and over his wispy brown hair she locked eyes with Richard.

She knew he was thinking the same thing she was.

Where is your mama, little one?

Harry was so young that he might not even remember Clarissa if she did not return soon.

He would have transferred all that unconditional, fervent affection to Augusta, and she hated herself for the fierce, shameful pleasure that accompanied this thought.

After Mrs. Kirby had wiped the children's sticky faces with a dampened serviette, Richard asked the nurse to take them to the carriage while he had a word with Augusta.

The nurse gave them both a single stern look over her shoulder that said louder than words, *Behave!*

Augusta's heart was in her throat as Richard approached her with an earnest expression on his face.

He pitied her.

He sensed how shaken she had been by his kiss, and he *pitied* her!

"Let us not make a piece of work of this, if you please!" she blurted out before he could open his mouth.

If he explained to her in the kind tone he used with the children that it is perfectly normal for a spinster lady to attach far more meaning to a gentleman's impulsive kiss of gratitude than he intended, she would scream.

He would go on to say that although he had great esteem for her, he could never think of her in *that* way.

She was utterly humiliated by what she was feeling.

She would *not* let him turn her into a lovesick ninny.

Richard's eyes searched her face.

Augusta's eyes, which were so warm with love for little Harry a mere moment ago, had grown distant. They focused on a point just above his left shoulder.

He should be relieved. He had, in fact, been about to utter that precise sentiment.

Let us not make a piece of work of this, if you please.

She had sounded so prim. So fussy. But she had surprised him that day. He knew of no other woman of his acquaintance who would have dealt with the situation with such brutal competence. She had looked like a lioness when she thrust her finger down little Harry's throat.

She *was* superb. Clarissa did not know Augusta at all if she could dismiss her as a dried-up old maid.

His feelings were in turmoil. Could he be *attracted* to this most redoubtable female?

No.

The answer must be *no.*

Not while the fate of her sister was so uncertain.

It was only natural that their emotions would be in turmoil at the moment.

He had been jilted by her sister; she had been saddled with her sister's children. And it was the time of the winter solstice—the season of Misrule, in the old tradition, when chaos reigned over the earth.

It was not surprising that neither was thinking clearly, with the very planets aligned against them.

He forced himself to smile.

"Always so sensible, Augusta," he said. "You relieve my mind."

"I am not a fool, my lord," she said.

"Richard," he reminded her as he raised her hand to his lips. She quickly snatched it away, and he gaped at her, feeling . . . hurt.

"Not that one," she said, practical to the core. "That's the one Harry, um . . . better have this one, instead."

Incredibly, she gave him her other hand.

The spell broken, he laughed out loud and then kissed it.

Six

Augusta eagerly broke the wax seal on the note from the registry office the next morning, but found that instead of a nurse, the office had found two prospective lady's maids for her consideration.

She brushed a self-conscious hand over her hair. She had been tying it back to keep it out of her way as she supervised the maids in their cleaning and the cook at her baking.

Certainly, her appearance could use some attention. The other female servants had done their best for her between their usual tasks in readying the house for so many guests, but the lady's maid who had served Augusta's mother and then herself after that lady's death had always pressed Augusta's gowns perfectly, and she knew exactly how to subdue the rebellious natural wave of her dark hair so it would stay perfectly in its chignon.

Augusta repressed the wistful thought that Richard was accustomed to women who knew every unnatural art to make themselves appear to advantage.

She was *not* one of the Marquess of Ardath's flirts.

On this glum note, she sent a message around to the registry office to say that she would be at home that day to interview the candidates, the first at ten o'-clock and the second at eleven.

The first candidate was so like the traitorous departed Crump that Augusta nearly engaged her on the spot. She was neat and dignified and spoke only when spoken to. Her references showed that she gave complete satisfaction for all the employers who had retained her through a long history of service dating from the time she was seventeen. She found herself in need of a situation now, she said in answer to Augusta's question, because her last mistress had died unexpectedly.

She could be ready to start work immediately.

Did Augusta imagine the slight curl of disapproval in the woman's face that made her acutely conscious of the slightly rumpled state of her gown and the wayward lock of hair that straggled at her cheek after breaking free of its moorings? Indeed, Crump never would have allowed her mistress to be seen in such a state, even if it was far in advance of calling hours.

Augusta opened her mouth to engage the woman, but found herself hesitating.

Crump, for all the excellence of her work, had turned tail and run without a backward look before the children had been in residence for two days. Augusta vividly remembered the maid's statement that children made her nervous and having them inflicted upon her in her old age was hardly a fitting reward for her long, faithful service to Augusta's family.

Faithful service, indeed!

The woman no doubt had savings, for she never spent a penny from what Augusta could see, and all of her living expenses were provided by her employer.

So she could well afford to flee Augusta's home at a moment's notice.

Well, Clarissa's children were coming back as soon as her holiday party was over, and, for all that it was unfair to assume that this woman would have the same reaction to their noise and unceasing demands for attention that Crump did, Augusta could see that she was cut from the very same cloth.

"How do you feel about children?" Augusta asked. "Three very young, very active children."

"Children?" the woman said, raising her brows in distaste. "The registry office said *nothing* about children."

"My niece and nephews," Augusta said. "My sister's children."

"I am a lady's maid," she said with a chilly smile that was no doubt meant to be conciliating. "I assume you employ a nurse to see to their needs, so they will not concern me."

"Thank you," Augusta said in polite dismissal as she stood. "I shall inform the registry office of my decision."

Since the applicant had very correctly stood throughout the interview, she merely bowed and took her departure.

When the second applicant presented herself a half hour later, Augusta was tempted to run for the registry office at once to beg the other woman to return.

The new applicant was young and pretty, and she inspected Augusta with bold, but not wholly critical blue eyes.

"I would crop your hair at once," she said before Augusta had voiced her first question. "It is much too attractive to wear all skinned back like that."

"Thank you," said Augusta, taken aback at so personal an observation. So impertinent a servant would not have been tolerated in her mother's household above a quarter of an hour. "May I ask why you have left your previous employer? I see by your references that you have been employed in just two previous households."

"Her son would not leave his eyes or his hands off of me," the girl said with unfeigned indignation. "I'm a good girl, I am. Besides, his mother caught wind of what was going on and gave me the sack."

"I see," Augusta said. "And your previous employer?"

"A tradesman's wife who thought I was good enough before her husband purchased a title," she said resentfully. "She gave me the sack so she could hire a fancy French maid with her long nose in the air. She will not get half the work out of her that she did out of me, I promise you."

"I see," Augusta said again as she started to stand.

The girl gave a long sigh.

"I'm not one to waste time regretting the past," she said, "but I miss the children."

"Children?" Augusta said, sitting back down abruptly.

"They were sweet little things," she said. "Reminded me of my own brothers and sisters at home, miss. You have never seen such a collection of noisy, sneaking little rascals, bless 'em."

Augusta felt her lips strain wide with a smile so avid and so eager that the girl blinked and stepped back a pace.

"When you can you start?" she asked.

Every piece of furniture in Augusta's house shone so brilliantly with beeswax that it looked as if it were surfaced with glass. The kissing boughs were so laden with fruits and dangling walnuts that they seemed about to topple to the gleaming hardwood floors.

The house smelled of clean pine from the branches that decorated the room, and of butter and cinnamon with brown sugar from the dazzling array of pastries spread on the side tables.

The dining room table was set with snowy damask and Augusta's grandmother's prized set of cream, gold, and ruby-red china. A large silver epergne overflowing with flowers, candies, and nutmeats was set in the precise center and flanked by a series of matching silver holders with white beeswax candles aflame.

Augusta's hair was newly cropped so her dark curls swirled attractively about her face, and she was wearing the gown her maid had insisted that she have made up for her from a bolt of frightfully expensive Italian brocade the hue of a ripe peach that Eliza spied in the shop where she had accompanied Augusta to purchase a pair of evening gloves.

Still, Augusta did not grudge the exorbitant expense the dressmaker commanded for making the gown so quickly. She had never looked so fine, if the unfamiliar image in her glass was any indication.

She had not seen Richard for two days, although Mrs. Kirby had brought the children to pay a short visit to her the day before.

"Pretty," Harry had said as he stroked her newly liberated curls and spoiled the artfully careless arrangement the new maid had been at such pains to achieve.

"Thank you, kind sir," Augusta had said as she gave him a gentle squeeze.

"Uncle Richard *will* want to marry you now," was Gerald's gleeful comment.

The thought made her giddy, even though it was absurd.

Once Clarissa returned, she would rarely see him. And if Clarissa did not return, well, he would have no reason to further involve himself in her affairs in that case, either.

The first of the ladies arrived, and Augusta stepped forward at once to greet them.

"Miss Oglethorpe!" said one of the elder, more well-to-do bluestockings as she regarded Augusta myopically through her spectacles. "Is that you? What have you done to yourself?"

"You look very fine," another said politely.

"Thank you," Augusta said, although she did not mistake the comment for a compliment. As the ladies trooped into her house and exclaimed over the decorations as they did every year, Augusta moved quickly about the room to make sure all of her guests were comfortable.

"Good Lord, is that a *kissing* bough?" one of the women said in disbelief as she looked overhead at the chandelier. She gave a cackle of laughter. She fancied herself quite the intellectual, and had taken to wearing mannish suits and carrying an ivory cane when she was quite a young woman. She had very little use for men because they were, in her opinion, the vile oppressors of her sex.

"Well, yes," Augusta said, taken aback.

"Very pretty," said another, more kindly woman.

"A symbol of the shackles with which men have enslaved us for thousands of years," the first woman declared.

"The oranges look delicious, though," the other

woman said wistfully. "I have not had an orange in twenty years."

"You will have one tonight," Augusta said, smiling gratefully at her for changing the subject as she greeted a very elderly guest, a famous lady scholar in her day whose eyes were now so weak from squinting at obscure texts that she had to be led by a younger, stouter friend to keep from walking into walls.

The scholar petted the soft silk brocade of Augusta's sleeve as if it were the face of a beloved friend.

"Pay no mind to Beatrice. She was a joyless old crank when she was twenty. I once had a gown made of fabric such as this," she said remininscently. "Wear this pretty gown while you can, gel. And get yourself a husband with it, too, if you can."

Ten pairs of eyes focused on the two of them in shock.

"I only say what the rest of you are thinking," the elderly woman said, raising her voice as if she could see the glares. Perhaps she could feel them.

The scholar patted Augusta's hand where it gently grasped her arm preparatory to helping her lower herself into a comfortable chair.

"Phoebe, I am sure I have never heard you utter such a sentiment in your life," said the elder lady's companion in disapproval. "You are gifted with a fine mind. Yours is a higher purpose beyond the mundane lot of women to breed children and wear themselves out catering to the whims of some man."

The old woman cackled with bitter amusement.

"*Was,*" she corrected her. "Mine *was* a higher purpose. But I am old and have only you, my faithful friend, and my musty old texts for company now that I can no longer see well enough to read them." She patted Augusta's hand again. "Such firm, pretty skin," she said with a sigh. "And such a generous nature to go with it. Do not waste the whole of your youth with a parcel of old antidotes like us, my dear Miss Oglethorpe. Go out and find yourself a man. A *good* one. There should still be some of them about."

The other ladies began to whisper among themselves in reaction to such heresy.

"You are not well," Clara, her companion, suggested.

"I am perfectly well, or as near to it as I ever am at my age," the scholar said. "They are staring at me, are they not? Well, the only good thing about being an outspoken old crow is I can say whatever I please."

"I will consider your advice," Augusta said diplomatically.

"Do that!" the old woman said gleefully. "Where are these famous oranges? I have a fancy to try one."

Thank heaven the marquess generously had sent over a large case of them as his contribution, his note said, to her party. They must have cost him a fortune! She watched in satisfaction as her dignified guests leaned over the dining table with their faces over their plates to catch any juice dripping from their chins. Her butler looked a trifle put out that they had departed from convention to eat oranges before he could have the footmen serve the fish soup, but Augusta did not care.

The conversation sparkled, and the room was filled with feminine laughter. The ladies enjoyed the meal prodigiously, as they always did. The lady scholar's remarks were on Augusta's mind throughout the meal, and she looked at some of her so-called friends with new eyes.

They resented her new appearance. They seemed . . . jealous.

Well, Augusta resented their resentment! How *dare* they raise their eyebrows to one another in silent commentary at her new hairstyle and fashionable gown?

She was still the same person inside.

Then she realized the truth.

She was *not* the same person inside.

All the while she received the grateful thanks of the genteelly impoverished ladies for the lovely meal and warm, cozy fire, all the while she forced her attention not to stray from the academic topics that once would have fascinated her, she felt a panic rise inside her.

This had always been the high point of her year, and now she couldn't wait for all these ladies to leave so she could see Richard and the children again.

Were they happy in Richard's house? Had she been selfish to accept his offer to take them off her hands while she prepared for the party?

Or were they *too* happy in Richard's house? Would they have grown so attached to him and Mrs. Kirby that they would not *want* to live with Augusta when the party was over?

Was Mrs. Kirby keeping a watchful eye on Harry so he would not eat anything dreadful? Was Cynthia bullying Gerald, as she was wont to do? Was Gerald climbing the furniture—he liked to sit up high—and in danger of falling and cracking his head open? Had Augusta remembered to warn Mrs. Kirby against this?

That was when it struck her—now that the children had entered her life, she could not go back to her old way of living it.

For better or for ill, her life had been irreparably changed.

Surreptitiously, she stole a glance at the clock on the mantel. Perhaps, if her guests left within the hour, she could get to Richard's house before the children were asleep. The women were sitting at the table, their meals pretty much consumed, enjoying the conversation.

They could just as easily talk in the parlor. And, once tea and more little cakes were served, they could be gently led to the idea of departure. She normally suggested music after the meal. One of the ladies was quite a talented pianist, and several others liked to sing. Augusta could simply fail to suggest it. The ladies were too polite to stay longer if Augusta subtly signaled that the evening was over, and it was time for them to go home.

But she looked around the table at the animated faces and simply could not do it.

Her friends, she knew, would simply go home with bluff good humor. This was by no means the high spot of *their* year.

But the elderly ones, the ones who had fallen on lean times in their middle age, would be disappointed.

No, Augusta could not serve them such a trick, she decided. She remained seated with a polite, attentive smile on her face, and resigned herself to waiting to see the children, and Richard, until tomorrow.

Seven

Richard's knees practically brushed his chin as he sat in one of the schoolroom chairs and watched Cynthia, her voice haughty with importance, serve imaginary tea in the small chipped cups from which he and his brother had drunk milk in this very room when they were small.

Cynthia was in her element playing society hostess.

"Will you have milk or sugar, my lord?" she asked in a perfect imitation of her mother's voice. Her back was straight, and her chin was raised. She was absolutely adorable.

"Both," he said. If she had offered hemlock with a smile like that, he would have drunk it gladly.

But then it was all pretend, like this comfortable illusion he had that his life was suspended in time at this moment in a state of perfect happiness and safety, and for this time, at least, no malevolent outside force could intrude.

Perhaps this is what it is to have a family, he mused, then chided himself for this mawkish sentimentality.

He had seen plenty of discordant marriages, and the arrival of children, he knew from the complaints of his cronies who had sought refuge from their families at their clubs, was no guarantee of domestic felicity.

Quite the contrary.

Children grew up to be rebellious adolescents. Wives and husbands grew apart and pursued their pleasures separately. Most of the married couples he knew barely managed to retain the veneer of civility in front of their guests at dinner parties. The best one could hope for was that a state of polite indifference would rule over the household once the demands of passion, or of duty to one's lineage, were satisfied.

He brought himself up short.

He had described precisely the life he would have lived with Clarissa. He had offered for her, knowing this.

Expecting this.

Gerald, parodying Richard's example, smiled and accepted a cup of imaginary tea from his sister. The little boy preened when Cynthia addressed him as Mr. Fenshaw.

Richard's grin was quite wiped from his face when Harry burst into tears. Richard shot to his feet at once and winced a little when he heard his knees creak.

"What is it, little fellow?" Richard said as he reached down and hoisted Harry to rest on his hip.

"Want Aunt 'Gusta," he pouted.

"Aunt Augusta is engaged this evening. We will pay a visit to her tomorrow."

With a jolt he realized that when they paid that visit, he would leave the children with Augusta. For good.

"Want Aunt 'Gusta *now,*" Harry said.

"Your Aunt Augusta is having a party at her house," Richard explained as he dried Harry's wet cheeks with his handkerchief.

"Just like Mama," Gerald said. "Mama had parties all

the time, and we stayed in the nursery, and then one day she ran away."

"Aunt 'Gusta ran away!" Harry cried in renewed distress.

"No, Aunt Augusta did *not* run away," Richard said. "She would *never* run away without telling you."

"Mama ran away," Gerald said matter-of-factly. "But she will be back by Christmas."

Richard, nonplussed, greeted the arrival of Mrs. Kirby and the children's dinner with relief. His old nurse was in the habit of supervising Richard's chef in the preparation of the children's food because she didn't trust the foreign artist not to put something heathenish in it that would prove insalubrious to a child's delicate constitution. She had done the same when Richard's parents ruled the household, and several cooks had given their notice because of it.

Cynthia still playing lady of the manor, grandly directed the servant accompanying Mrs. Kirby in the placement of the food on the small table. Her little face was set, and Richard realized that she had her own way of dealing with her mother's disappearance.

"Come along, Master Harry," said Mrs. Kirby when Harry failed to come to the table at Cynthia's imperious request. "It is time to eat your dinner."

"Not hungry," he said, looking like a small brown-haired mule. "Want Aunt 'Gusta."

"He did not eat his breakfast, either," Mrs. Kirby said. Her brow was furrowed with concern. "And he ate barely enough at dinner last night to keep a bird alive."

"Why was I not told this?" Richard demanded. Was it his imagination, or did Harry suddenly look thinner?

Mrs. Kirby gave him a look of astonishment.

"One does not disturb the master with such things."

"This master, you do," he told her. "Harry, my boy. Just a few bites to please me. Look here." In desperation, he picked up one of the spoons and rashly took a bite of the cooling porridge. Mrs. Kirby was a staunch believer in porridge for children.

"Delicious," Richard declared as the gummy substance adhered itself to his teeth. It tasted like glue, just as he remembered it. Mrs. Kirby had not lost her talent for turning the most promising foodstuffs into something one could use to seal the cracks between the bricks in a garden wall, confident that even the insects would scorn to gnaw at it.

Harry was not fooled.

"Want Aunt 'Gusta," he cried, and burst into tears.

Richard looked from one small face to another. Harry's tearful one. Gerald's solemn one. Cynthia's set one. That was the one that broke his heart.

"I know a house where the hostess has oranges and walnuts and little cakes baked with sugar and cinnamon, and a roasted goose so big that four more mouths to feed would be as nothing to her," he said.

Harry and Gerald looked at him blankly.

"She does not want us there," Cynthia said, tossing her blonde curls.

"Yes, she does," he said, with absolute conviction. "She wants you very much."

With that, he ordered Mrs. Kirby and the servant to take the dinner away and dress the children in their best clothes.

They were going to a party.

Richard signaled the children for silence as he put out his arm to stop them from bursting into Augusta's parlor. The butler had admitted them without hesitation, but Richard could hardly permit the children to rush into the room while the performers were in the middle of a song.

A dark-haired lady in peach brocade played the harp, while an older woman played the piano. All he could see of the younger lady's face was the curve of her cheek and the graceful nape of her neck. A third lady with a sweet, true voice that quavered only slightly on the high notes sang an Italian aria.

He looked around the room for Augusta in the hope that he could catch her eye, but he did not see her. Then his eyes returned to the dark-haired harpist.

No, his eyes had not deceived him. It was Augusta, and she looked beautiful, like an angel, at her harp. His mouth dropped open.

"Aunt 'Gusta," cried Harry, and ran on stout little legs to throw himself at her. Richard, distracted by the angelic vision she presented at the harp, made a grab for the boy a moment too late.

The harp gave a discordant screech as Augusta looked down and stared at the child. Then a radiant smile burst upon her face and she hauled him into her lap to give him a big smacking kiss. The vocalist, who had stopped singing, reached out to steady the harp before it could topple over on the floor.

"Harry, darling," Augusta cried. "Whatever are you doing here?" She became conscious of the whispers and faced her guests. "My nephew, Harry," she said, smiling at them. She looked up to see Richard, resplendent in black evening dress, place a restraining hand on Gerald's shoulder.

Cynthia had already flounced into the room in her fussy pink dress and beamed winsomely at the pianist.

"I always sing for Mama's guests," she said.

"Of course you do, my dear," the pianist said, utterly charmed. "What would you like to sing?"

Richard placed a wooden chair near the piano and lifted the little girl onto the seat so everyone could see her. He kept a protective hand on her shoulder.

"My niece, Cynthia," Augusta said for the benefit of her guests as she beckoned to Gerald, who was still standing by the doorway, looking uncertain. When he ran up to her, she put her arm on the boy's shoulders and kissed him on the cheek. He leaned against her.

Cynthia began to sing, and one of the middle-aged bluestockings squinted through a quizzing glass similar to that carried by men.

"Richard!" she demanded imperiously. "Is that *you?*"

"Good evening, Aunt Elvira," he said, looking sheepish. Miss Elvira Steen was no blood relation to him, actually, but a friend of his late mother. She had quite doted on him and his brother before she had turned her back on her conventional family to lead a solitary life in London with her fellow bluestockings.

Cynthia broke off her song and glared at the woman.

"I am *singing,*" Cynthia said indignantly.

"I beg your pardon, my dear," the lady said, struggling to keep a straight face. "Pray continue."

"Let us start from the beginning, shall we?" suggested the pianist.

Cynthia gave a gracious inclination of her head, and complied.

The song was a simple romantic ballad, not entirely suitable for a child, Augusta thought, but Cynthia sang it in her childish soprano without missing a word or a note. Richard smiled broadly at her all the while, just as if he were a proud papa.

The elder ladies were nodding with the music. One of the younger ladies, whom Augusta had considered one of her closest friends until that moment, raised her eyebrows in arch disapproval and whispered something to the woman sitting next to her.

"That was lovely, Cynthia," said Augusta when the child was finished with her song and curtsied prettily to the company. Richard picked her up off the chair, gave her a kiss on the cheek, and put her down so she could run to join Gerald and Harry, who had gone to sit in front-row chairs beside Miss Steen. Cynthia accepted a kiss from Augusta, but leaned closer to Richard.

Augusta sighed.

To her surprise, her erstwhile friend, Dorothea, stood and led the way as several of her weaker-willed companions scuttled after her with apologetic looks toward Augusta.

"Excuse me," Augusta said to the rest of her guests, and followed. "Dorothea, you need not leave so early," Augusta said.

"I had no idea this was to become a nursery party," Dorothea said stiffly.

"My sister's children are part of my life now," Augusta said, feeling strangely serene when she should be mourning this long-standing friendship that was apparently at an end. "If you want to continue to be a part of my life, you must accept their presence in it."

"I think not," Dorothea said, curling her lip, and left.

"*Et tu,* Susan?" Augusta said to the woman who prepared to follow Dorothea out the door.

"It's for the best," she said. The smile she gave Augusta was pitying.

To Augusta's consternation, several others followed.

"Do call on me when you are not so occupied, my dear," one of them said, and pressed her hand.

"Miss Carter?" Augusta said in surprise. This lady had applauded loudest for Cynthia's performance.

"I came with Dorothea," she said, looking wistful. "I should have liked to stay."

"I should be pleased to take you home in my carriage, madam," Richard said quietly as he put his warm hands on Augusta's bare shoulders. She had not heard him approach.

Miss Carter's wrinkled face lit up.

"Oh, thank you, my lord," she said happily as she returned to the parlor.

"You look beautiful," Richard said to Augusta, now that they were alone.

She smiled tremulously.

"You look beautiful, too," she told him.

Beautiful was an understatement. The sight of Richard in full evening dress made her knees weak.

He laughed. Then his smile faded and he looked up at the kissing bough that was suspended from the chandelier above them. He put one hand on her cheek and drew closer.

"You must come into the parlor at once," said a bossy, childish voice from the doorway. "I am going to sing again."

Cynthia stood there with her hands on her hips. Harry was beside her. He had his finger in his mouth.

With a rueful smile, Richard drew back from Augusta.

"Later," he whispered, and Augusta quivered with anticipation when he placed his hand at the small of her back and escorted her back into the parlor.

Eight

All of Augusta's guests were gone, and Harry, sitting contentedly in Augusta's lap, ate ravenously of cold roasted goose and bread. Gerald and Cynthia shared the last orange, and Richard and Augusta were drinking the spiced punch left from the party.

The candles were guttering in their holders.

"Mrs. Kirby will give me a rare dressing-down for keeping the children up so late," Richard said ruefully.

Augusta smiled at him.

"I am so glad you brought them," she said. "Dear Harry." She ruffled the child's hair and he smiled greasily at her. "What an appetite you have!"

"Are we going to live here with you now?" asked Gerald.

"No!" Cynthia cried. "I want to live with Uncle Richard! He told us he was to be our papa before Mama left."

"But, darling, that has changed. Your place is with me," Augusta said firmly.

"We should stay with Aunt 'Gusta," said Gerald. "Mama left us at this house. When she comes home, she will look for us here."

"Stay with Aunt 'Gusta," Harry said with satisfaction in his voice. He turned and put his head on

Augusta's bosom, much to the peril of her Italian silk gown.

She didn't care.

"Aunt 'Gusta does not want us," Cynthia said, chin hardened.

"I do want you," Augusta said, and meant it. "The three of you are all I have . . ." *left of my sister,* Augusta had almost said. "That is, you are my only family except for your mother. Gerald is right. When she comes back, she will expect to find you here."

"You cared more for that stupid cat that ran away than you do for us," Cynthia scoffed.

"That is not true!" Augusta said.

"Mama will come home in time for Christmas," Gerald said, but it sounded as if he were trying to convince himself as much as the others. "She said she would come back and bring us a nice surprise."

A nice surprise. Augusta and Richard glanced at each other with dismay. The "surprise," no doubt, was a new papa. Him.

But instead, Clarissa had disappeared. Augusta was more convinced than ever that something dreadful had happened to her.

"I will send to Bow Street again tomorrow," Richard said quietly, and Augusta nodded in grateful acceptance.

Cynthia cried a little when Richard left without her, but her eyes were dry and hard when she turned to face Augusta.

"I hate you," she said. "You made him go away."

"It is late. Lord Ardath has his own home to go to."

"Will he come to see us tomorrow?" asked Gerald.

"Perhaps," Augusta said. "I hope so."

"You want to marry him yourself," Cynthia said. "You do not care if Mama does not come back."

"I care. Very much," Augusta said, striving to hold on to her patience. "It is time for all of you to go to bed. Lord Ardath will send over the rest of your things tomorrow."

"Mama will be home for Christmas," said Gerald.

"Uncle Richard was going to teach us to ice skate," Cynthia said.

At that moment, Augusta's new maid came into the room.

"The children are here," she said excitedly. Then she looked embarrassed. "Beg pardon, miss."

"It is quite all right," Augusta said, glad for the interruption.

"It will be a proper Christmas now, with children in the house," the girl said. "I'll take that one for you, miss," she said, indicating Harry, who, now replete, was asleep on her lap.

"No," Augusta said, touching his baby-fine brown hair. She wasn't ready to give him up yet. "I will take him up myself."

The maid nodded and herded Gerald and Cynthia from the room before her.

"I am surprised you did not become a nursemaid rather than a lady's maid," Augusta said later as the maid brushed her short curls in preparation for bed. "You seem so fond of children."

"*Anyone* can take care of children," the odd little maid said grandly. "My talent is transforming sows' ears into silk purses. All of my mistresses were the better for it once *I* took them in hand."

All two of them, Augusta thought, choosing to be amused rather than offended by the girl's frankness.

It was clear she thought of Augusta as one of her challenges.

"I know nothing about children," Augusta admitted.

"It will be all right, miss," the girl said with that unshakable confidence that made her at once so disconcerting and so comfortable. "I know *everything.*"

Richard arrived on Augusta's doorstep at an unfashionably early hour of the day with several pairs of ice skates in his hands.

"Uncle Richard!" cried Cynthia when she saw the ice skates. "You *remembered!*"

"I never forget any promise I make to a pretty girl," he said.

She ran straight to him and clamped her arms around his knees, which almost caused him to topple over.

"How very kind," Augusta said, beaming at him. "Look, Gerald, Harry. Lord Ardath has come to take you ice skating!"

"The pond in the park is frozen. We could not have a more perfect day," Richard said.

"I shall have Eliza fetch the children's coats," Augusta said.

"Have her fetch yours, too," Richard said, dangling a pair of skates before her.

"But I—no, Richard. I am afraid I do not skate. I have not done so since I was child."

"Well, neither have I," he said, lowering his voice. "If *I* am going to make a cake of myself before the whole of London, you are going to be right beside me."

She looked at the three little faces watching her. Harry and Gerald looked hopeful. Cynthia regarded her with cool eyes. Richard was grinning at her, like the devil she once had thought him.

This was a test.

"Very well, then," she said. "I will have Eliza come along, too, in order to help with the children."

"Eliza said she will have Aunt 'Gusta married to the marquess before the cat can lick her ear," said Gerald. "Does she mean *you*, Uncle Richard?"

"Uncle Richard is going to marry Mama," said Cynthia, tossing her blonde curls. "And we are all going to live with Uncle Richard in his house."

"There, Gerald," said Augusta dryly. "You have your answer."

The park, to Richard's dismay, was full of people. There were festive colored lanterns placed all about the edge of the pond, presumably so skaters could continue to enjoy their exercise after the sun began to set. A small band composed of a violinist, a drummer, and two horn players played sprightly music, with a hat placed on the ground for tips.

Two of Richard's cronies stopped to laugh at him as he lurched awkwardly about on his skates.

"Cutting a dashing figure on the ice, are you, Ardath? Haven't seen you at the club for an age," one of them said. "The fair Fenshaw's brats, are they?"

"Mrs. Fenshaw's children, yes," Richard said defensively.

"What happened? Did the woman disappear and leave them on your hands? Flighty little baggage, that, though pretty enough."

Richard glared at the speaker.

"Mrs. Fenshaw had a pressing engagement out of

town. The children are awaiting her return at their aunt's house," he said repressively. "Not that it is any of *your* business."

"Oh, beg pardon," the man said, taking a step back at his fierce expression. "Of course. See you at the club, then."

He touched the brim of his hat to Augusta, and left.

"Gossips worse than an innkeeper's wife," Richard muttered.

He was holding hands with Gerald and Cynthia, but, truth be told, he was relying more on their support than they were relying on his.

"This is fun!" Gerald cried as he broke free and skated a few competent steps by himself.

Deprived of the balance of the child at his left side, Richard staggered and toppled over like a felled tree, dragging a screeching Cynthia down with him. He quickly twisted so he landed with an arm braced on either side of the child so he wouldn't crush her.

To his utter humiliation, Augusta helped him to his feet and skated gracefully away in an ever-widening circle around him.

Her cheeks were pink and her dark curls danced beneath her hat.

He brushed the snow from his damp clothes and almost fell over again.

"Are you all right, Uncle Richard?" asked Gerald, who lurched to an untidy stop beside him.

"Perfectly," Richard said. The maid, Eliza, swooped down on Gerald and towed him over to Augusta, who was holding hands with Harry. Then she came to fetch Cynthia, and arranged her on the other side of Harry.

"Come along, Uncle Richard," cried Cynthia. "We are going to form a daisy chain! It will be fun."

Richard made his way toward them with excruciating slowness. It might be faster, he observed bitterly to himself, if he simply gave in to the inevitable and crawled on his hands and knees.

Augusta hoisted Harry to her hip and skated over to Richard.

"Take my hand," she said, reaching out to him. She gave him a look of mock sympathy. Her lovely dark eyes were dancing with mischief. "We will go very slowly at first."

"I thought you had not skated since you were a child," he said reproachfully. He grabbed her gloved hand as if it were a lifeline.

"And so I have not," she said. "I have not enjoyed myself so much in years. I am so glad you invited me to come with you and the children."

"So am I," he said, grinning back at her. He looked at the maid, Cynthia, and Gerald, all holding hands and waiting for them. "Maybe I had better watch you instead. I probably will pull you all down," he said ruefully.

"You cannot get out of it now," she said. "The children would be disappointed. They are afraid you are not enjoying yourself because you keep falling down."

He saw then that Cynthia and Gerald were watching him with looks of anxiety on their faces.

"Nonsense," he said stoutly. "That is half the fun."

"You have the heart of a hero," she said with glowing eyes. He could not detect a trace of mockery in them. She towed him to the place where the others were waiting

Richard took Gerald's hand, and the boy's face lit up as if from within. A big smile spread over his face.

"*I* want to hold Uncle Richard's hand," Cynthia said jealously.

To maintain the peace, Augusta suggested that Richard be placed between the two children so they could both hold onto his hands, and Augusta, at the head of the daisy chain with her maid, led the unwieldy group forward. Richard was enchanted by the sound of her laughter echoing over her shoulder, and tried not to laugh too loudly or too long, once he was certain she and Harry were uninjured, when she missed her footing and went sprawling. She had the foresight to twist around so that Harry landed on top. She sat up with her hat dipped drunkenly over one eye.

By the time Richard had lurched to Augusta's side, the sturdy little maid already had scooped up Harry and hauled Augusta to her feet by one arm.

"Nothing broken?" he asked Augusta as he struggled to remain upright.

"I do not think so," Augusta said, laughing up into his eyes. "But my limbs are so numb from the cold, I might find a bruise or two when I thaw them out."

Richard noticed then that the children's noses were cherry red. Harry's lips were actually a bit blue at the edges.

"I think it is time for us to go inside," he said, and watched their smiles fade. Cynthia's face had formed the beginnings of a pout when inspiration struck.

He bent down to speak conspiratorially to the little girl.

"My chef, Pierre," he said as if he were confiding an important secret, "makes the finest hot chocolate in all of London. He mixes it with vanilla and cream, and he puts little candied cherries on the top. And I have it on good authority that he spent all of yesterday baking those little tarts with brown sugar and cinnamon in them that you and Gerald like so much, and threw a proper tantrum when he learned you had gone to live with your Aunt Augusta before he could give them to you. I think it would make Pierre very happy if you would all come home with me and eat some of them now, do you not agree?"

The smiles magically reappeared.

"Yes," cried Cynthia, clapping her hands. "I am very fond of Pierre's tarts."

"I will just go along home, then, shall I, miss?" asked the maid very properly. She would not be needed now that they were to leave the ice. But her blue eyes were wistful.

"Nonsense," Richard said genially. Some part of him was appalled by the way he reveled in this patriarch business. He touched his hat and nodded to a sporting acquaintance who stared at him with mouth agape. "It is a long, cold walk back to Miss Oglethorpe's house. You must come with us and have some hot chocolate, too."

After they had removed their skates and started to move toward Richard's coach, they found their way barred by a familiar little middle-aged lady, who squinted myopically at them.

"Richard? Is that *you?*" she said in disbelief. "I thought I recognized you and Miss Oglethorpe out on the ice, but I made sure I was mistaken."

"It is I, Aunt Elvira," he said, beaming at her in an excess of goodwill. "Come along with us, if you please. Pierre is going to make hot chocolate."

"With vanilla and cream with candied cherries on top," Augusta said, grinning as she linked arms with the bewildered bluestocking and gently turned her around to lead her with them to the carriage.

"And tarts!" said Gerald happily.

"I do believe I will," she said with a shrewd glance at her honorary nephew. "I say, Richard. You are like those swans that look so graceful on the water, but are so awkward on land, only in reverse."

"Thank you, Aunt Elvira," he said dryly, but he felt a big, silly grin spread over his face.

Nine

Augusta's mouth dropped open when the marquess's butler opened the front door of his home to them.

From its address in one of the oldest and most prestigious areas in Mayfair, she had known it would be large and well-appointed, but she had not been prepared for anything so . . . grand.

Yet, she decided as she faced the ocean of gleaming black and white marble that led into the heart of the imposing mansion, it suited him. Or, at least, it suited the marquess she had first met when he was flirting with her sister several months ago.

She had disapproved of him then. Now she was not sure she approved of this house.

It was beautiful but cold, like she had once thought him.

"I see you've kept your father's house," his Aunt Elvira said. She raised her voice and called, "Hallooooo—ooooooo" so it would echo down the cavernous expanse of the room.

Gerald, delighted, imitated her.

"Gerald," Augusta exclaimed, "you must not make so much noise."

It seemed rude, somehow, to disturb the solemn tone of the house, as if one were shouting in church.

"Nonsense," Richard said, patting the boy on the head when he looked uncertain. "Can't think what else having such a mausoleum of a house is good for. Go now with Eliza, children, and find Mrs. Kirby. She will be delighted to see you. Tell her I wish for her and Eliza to join us in the red parlor. I shall have a word with Pierre."

Cynthia, Gerald, and Harry took Eliza's hands and went clattering off toward the grand stairway punctuated with graceful classical statuary and the gracious patina of antique silver vases. The vases were empty of flowers, as Augusta might have expected, for no lady presided over this household.

It made her think, painfully, of Clarissa, who was meant to be its mistress.

"Please show the ladies to the red parlor," Richard said to the butler, who bowed and escorted Augusta and Miss Steen to a beautiful room half paneled in dark mahogany. The rest of the room, as expected, was painted a warm, dramatic shade of carnelian red. The furniture was made in the Egyptian style, upholstered in black and carnelian with sphinxes carved on the chair arms and carved crocodile claws for legs. The surfaces of the tables gleamed with inlaid onyx squares.

"Come along, Augusta," Miss Steen said when Augusta stood, blinking, for a moment, on the threshold. She seated herself on the sofa. "It is quite comfortable, and is Richard's favorite room. He had it decorated to suit himself shortly after he came to the title. The rest he left as it was in his grandfather's day, as did his father before him."

"It is quite impressive," Augusta said. "Perhaps we should not permit the children—"

"Nonsense. There is little a child can harm in here."

Augusta was too polite to argue with a lady so many years her senior, but she doubted Miss Steen had any conception of just how destructive three small children could be. They had certainly left an indelible impression on *her* house. Since she had no nursery apartments, the children had made free with her parlor with drastic results. Neither the carpeting nor her white brocade sofa would ever be the same. And not even the most aggressive remedies employed by the maids could eradicate the scratches made with some hard implement on the table.

"How long have you and Richard had this understanding?" Elvira asked into the silence.

"Understanding? I do not know what you mean."

"I have not seen that boy laugh so much in years. Why would he escort a female and a passel of children about London if he were not head over heels in love?"

"He is not in love with *me,*" Augusta said, feeling her face flush with embarrassment. It had not occurred to her that anyone would think such a thing.

"Nonsense. As a rule, he pays a visit to me during the first week of December and presents me with a handsome gift. This year it was a mantel clock. Then he disappears until after the New Year. Christmas is next week. Yet here in London he remains, making a spectacle of himself on ice skates for the pleasure of an unmarried lady and her niece and nephews. Richard has spent every Christmas since his brother's death in seclusion despite the many invitations extended to him. Five years it has been now. It is well past time he has stopped blaming himself."

"What happened to the marquess's brother?" Augusta asked.

"Killed in action. He was a cavalry officer."

"But how could Lord Ardath possibly blame himself for that?"

"I signed his death warrant," Richard said quietly from the doorway.

"What utter nonsense," said Miss Steen roundly. "You purchased a pair of colors for him. The boy was army mad, and he would have enlisted, else."

"My father refused to buy him a commission. He said he had only the two sons left after the deaths of my mother and elder brothers in infancy, and he would not risk either of them. When he died and I inherited the title, I gave in to Arthur's entreaties and purchased the commission for him. It was my first official act as marquess. To send my brother to his death."

"You could not have known."

"I have been surrounded by death all my life. How could I *not* have known?"

At that moment, the children clattered into the room. Cynthia and Gerald ran straight to Richard and began jostling each other and vying for his attention. Harry, with his thumb in his mouth, went to Augusta.

She would have to cure Harry of that, she thought as she patted him on the head. Her mother used to put some bitter substance on Clarissa's thumb to discourage her from sucking it. Perhaps Eliza would know what that would be. Or Mrs. Kirby, of course.

Both female servants now stood at the door, and Richard indicated with a slight inclination of his head that they were to enter and be seated.

Pierre himself brought the hot chocolate, an unprecedented act of condescension that made Elvira's eyes lift almost to the hairline of her steel-gray curls.

"The first cup for my beautiful Miss Cynthia," he said in his thick accent as he poured the fragrant beverage into a dainty porcelain cup.

Another surprising tribute.

Pierre usually affected to speak only French, particularly when he was displeased. Richard had always suspected he could speak English perfectly when it suited his purpose. Now he had proof.

That accomplished, Pierre made a slight bow and left the rest of the company to be served by one of the ladies. A maid who had entered the room in his wake put a platter filled with scrumptious looking little tarts and cakes on the table, and left when Richard nodded dismissal.

"If you would help the other children, Mrs. Kirby?" Richard said. He seemed quite restored to good humor. "And if you would pour for us, Miss Oglethorpe?"

"Certainly," Augusta said.

She had just taken a sip of the thick, creamy chocolate when the butler came to the doorway of the room and discreetly caught the marquess's attention. Augusta could see the underlying concern beneath the butler's impassive countenance.

The marquess apparently saw it, too, and hastily excused himself from his guests.

After a moment, the butler returned.

"Miss Oglethorpe. His lordship requires your presence at once. If you will follow me?"

"Of course," she said. Her heart was racing. It must be some news of Clarissa, and from the grim look on the butler's face, it would not be good news.

Richard was in the vestibule of his house, wearing

his coat and hat. He was in the act of drawing on his gloves, but when Augusta joined him, he let them drop to the floor and seized her hands.

"What is it?" she said, chilled by the look in his eyes.

"The runners think they have found her," he said. "A young, dark-haired woman of a suitable age has been drawn from the river. I must go at once to . . . see to it."

"It should be me," Augusta said. "She was . . . *is* my sister. I will go."

"No. She was to be my wife. It is *my* responsibility."

"It might not be she."

"In all likelihood it is not," he agreed, but she saw the sad resignation in his eyes.

He believed it was Clarissa.

And if it was, he would blame himself for her death, the same way he blamed himself for his brother's death.

"Stay with the children," he said. "Take them to your house when they have drunk their hot chocolate. And take Mrs. Kirby as well. It will take all of us to comfort them, if—"

"No," she said, holding her hand to his lips in order to keep the dreadful words from escaping. "Do not say it. Do not *think* it."

"I will come to you with news as soon as I can," he said as he gave her hands a final, bracing squeeze.

"I think you should know," Augusta said, "that there is a birthmark, a small one, in the shape of a—"

Richard gave her a bleak smile.

"In roughly the shape of a bell. Just below her left shoulder blade. I know."

Augusta bit her lip.

Of course he knew.

He had expected to marry her. And now he was prepared to claim her dead body.

Ten

Augusta did not know how she got through the rest of that afternoon and evening. Her nerves were raw with the effort of pretending all was well in front of the children.

The marquess had been called away on sudden urgent business, she told the children when they asked for him. After a while, they stopped asking, for Mrs. Kirby and Eliza did a splendid job of distracting them. Now the children were in bed, and Augusta had sent the exhausted nurse and maid to bed as well.

Restlessly, Augusta prowled the parlor and drank strong tea. And she forced herself to eat some toast.

She would need all the strength she could get if the news turned out to be grim.

Her heart leaped into her throat when she heard the door knocker. She rudely overtook her butler and thrust herself before him so she could throw the door open to him herself.

In the darkness of winter, he was nothing but a shadow. The gaslights illuminated the soft layer of snow on the top of his hat. He removed it and stepped inside.

The butler moved in deftly and nipped the hat from his hand. Then he left them alone.

The marquess's face was pale, and his mouth was grim.

Augusta could not speak. It seemed he suffered from the same affliction.

Then he relaxed his mouth into a solemn smile of relief and shook his head.

"It was not Clarissa," Augusta said, letting out all her breath at once. She sat down abruptly on a chair in the hall.

"No," he said, leaning above her and taking her hands. They were as cold as his. "The body was not . . . quite intact, but it was not Clarissa. I am certain of that."

"Thank heaven."

"I, too, am glad of it," he said, "but I can hardly rejoice when I know that somewhere a family mourns for this woman and may never discover what happened to her."

"You are a better person than I," she said. "It is selfish of me, but *I* can rejoice."

"You did not see her," he said.

His voice broke on the last word, and Augusta stood and put her arms around him. Her cheek rested against the snow-dampened wool of his greatcoat. He smelled faintly of bay rum and the winter night.

They stood like that for quite some time. Then they broke self-consciously apart.

"The children are well?" he asked. "They did not suspect my errand?"

"They are asleep. Cynthia has nightmares, did you know?"

"The boys do, too. Mrs. Kirby has gone to check on them and found them whimpering in their sleep. They do not remember the dreams in the morning."

"What are we to do with them?" Augusta asked plaintively.

He took her hands again.

"We will take care of them," he said firmly, "as long as they need us."

The next day, Augusta's bluestocking friends Dorothea and Susan came to call and stood in the doorway to the parlor with shock frozen on their faces when they discovered Augusta and the Marquess of Ardath engaged in a noisy board game spread messily upon the parlor table. Two little boys were shrieking with glee and a little girl was pouting. Apparently she had been the loser in whatever contest was in progress.

"Dorothea! Susan! I am so pleased that you have come," Augusta said, rising at once. "Do come in!"

"I will take the children for a walk," the marquess said, bowing politely to the visitors after introductions were performed. "I am certain the three of you would appreciate a quiet conversation away from these little demons."

He ruffled Gerald's hair affectionately, hoisted Harry to his hip and coaxed a pouting Cynthia out the door.

Dorothea watched them all go in blank astonishment.

"If I had not seen it with my own eyes, I would not have believed it!" she said. "He must be very much in love with your sister to take such an interest in her children. Have you received any word of her?"

Augusta had confided the truth of her sister's disappearance to her two closest friends, although Society in general believed Augusta's hastily concocted invention of a relative by marriage to whose sickbed Clarissa had been called on short notice.

"None," Augusta said, feeling ashamed. She had not thought of Clarissa for hours. Her heart and mind had been filled with Richard and the children and . . . joy, she realized.

"A very great pity," Susan said, covering Augusta's hand with her own. "I know this disruption in the routine of your household must be very disconcerting."

"Yes," Augusta said. "Very."

"I remember how distraught you were the day after your sister left them here," Dorothea said. "How absolutely dreadful for you!"

She knew that Dorothea and Susan could not possibly understand the transformation her feelings had undergone since then, so she merely nodded.

"I have come," Dorothea said handsomely, "to apologize for my behavior at your party. It was very rude of me to walk out on the entertainment. It was plain that you had not planned for that pert child to force herself on the company, and I should not have blamed you for it. I was disappointed. I had looked forward to an evening of good food and rational conversation. It was badly done of me." She looked down at her hands. "Your life may never return to normal if your sister does not return, and it is not the act of a friend to abandon you in your time of adversity. The least I can do is give you a half hour of my time now and again so you will be exposed to *some* rational conversation while you adjust to your . . . new circumstances."

Dorothea meant well, Augusta knew, but she made it sound as if the addition of her niece and nephews to her life was a catastrophe of epic proportions, in a class with being left penniless by a cruel fate or becoming an invalid.

Indeed, at first she had thought the same herself.

"It is very kind of you to come today, Dorothea," she said warmly. "And Susan," she added to the other lady.

"We especially wanted to remind you that we are to meet with the others on Tuesday next at Miss Watson's house to discuss Mr. Southey's excellent *Life of Nelson*. I do hope you will come. We missed you very much this week. You always have such interesting insights to share with us."

"Oh, but I have not read the work," Augusta said, "so I would not have much to contribute to the discussion." Indeed, Augusta had purchased Mr. Southey's book shortly before Clarissa left the children at her house, and she had forgotten all about it. "I have been so busy with the children—" she began.

Dorothea fixed a stern, but kindly look upon her.

"Augusta, my dear," she said firmly. "You must not allow your brain to deteriorate merely because you have been visited by adversity. These children who have taken over your life are your *sister's* responsibility. Hire a competent nurse to deal with them until the matter of your sister is resolved one way or another and continue, in the meantime, to proceed as you have always done."

"And *then* what? Give them over to the parish? Or simply keep them confined with their nurse and pretend they do not exist? You know nothing of children if you think that would be possible!"

"Nonsense. I was reared in such a manner myself, as was Susan, I am certain. As, I am sure you know, are most children of parents of the polite classes. Your sister, much as it pains me to speak ill of her when her fate is not known, did not rear her children to be studious and well-behaved. It is a sad reality that any ninnyhammer with a womb is capable of bearing children. You and I and Susan were meant for higher purposes."

"Higher purposes! To sit in a room and impress one another with our learned discussions? Cynthia, Gerald, and Harry are ages four, three, and two, and they may have lost their mother. My highest purpose right now is to comfort them in any way I can."

"And the Marquess of Ardath," Dorothea said archly. "No doubt he needs comforting as well."

"He meant to marry my sister," Augusta said. She felt her face flush. "Of course he is concerned."

"Concerned! One would think *he* were the children's guardian! And look at *you!* I suppose you had a sudden impulse to have your hair cropped in the latest style and purchase a wardrobe of fashionable clothes."

"It is my new maid," Augusta said. Her pretty white day gown with its fluttering periwinkle blue ribbons had come from the dressmaker only that morning. "She insisted."

"Now you are being bullied by a *maid?*" Susan said, laughing. "My dear Augusta. How absurd!"

"You do not know how hard it is to hire a maid at this season," Augusta said resentfully. "All of the unemployed girls go home to their families for Christmas. My maid left me without notice two days after Clarissa left the children here. She had grown old in my mother's and now my service, and her nerves were completely shattered by all the noise and confusion. I was fortunate to find a good-natured young girl who likes children to serve as my maid, and if doing things to my hair and choosing fabric for my gowns will keep her contented enough to stay, I shall not complain."

"All your maid's doing, then," Dorothea said with a faint, pitying smile on her face. "I saw the way you looked at the man, Augusta."

"Be fair, my dear," said Susan. "Augusta would have to be half dead *not* to look at *that* man in such a way. I had a good, long look at him myself. As did *you,* Dorothea. Admit it."

"Susan!" cried Dorothea, shocked.

"Oh, don't pucker up your face like that at *me,*" Susan said with a chuckle. "The marquess is very, very handsome. And that smile is enough to make even the most sensible woman lose her head." Susan leaned forward earnestly. "What we are saying, dear Augusta, is that you must not make a fool of yourself over the Marquess of Ardath. It has already started. You have neglected your reading and have stopped coming to our meetings—and for what?"

"For the sake of my sister's children," Augusta said. "The marquess is fond of them and has been kind enough to hire Bow Street Runners to search for their mother. That is all there is between us."

Dorothea and Susan exchanged pitying looks.

"My poor dear," said Dorothea, rising. "Please know that you can call upon either of us at any time."

"We are to meet on Tuesday next," Susan reminded Augusta. "Do come. You must not lose ties with the higher part of your intellect."

Augusta rose as well, and extended her hand. "I will remember," she said. "Tuesday next."

But she would not attend, she realized as she showed her friends to the door.

She was no longer the Augusta they knew. Indeed, she did not know herself anymore.

Once her friends had gone, she sat alone in the parlor, mechanically setting the game pieces back into their positions and replacing the scattered sofa cushions into their proper places. She held one pillow to her chest for comfort. Clarissa had embroidered it one long ago Christmas when she was seventeen. The design was of an angel in flight and blowing a horn.

That was before she and Clarissa had grown apart. Soon after, Clarissa met the man she would marry and Augusta, she realized now, had been jealous of Clarissa's new love and importance in the family circle. Augusta had endured the prenuptial parties and the wedding itself with all the inevitable jesting about her failure, as eldest, to marry first. After that, Clarissa and her husband started their family and left town for his father's house in York.

Augusta remembered now how much she had loved her pretty, dark-haired, sweet-natured little sister, and how Clarissa had followed her, the eldest and natural leader of the pair, everywhere when they were children.

Any ninnyhammer with a womb can bear children, Dorothea had said in a voice dripping with contempt. Indeed, Augusta had thought the same herself when she dutifully paid a visit to Clarissa upon the birth of each child. Clarissa had been radiant. Triumphant. *Smug,* was Augusta's interpretation of Clarissa's joyful reaction to having survived the ordeal of childbed.

She had been jealous, Augusta admitted. Jealous because Clarissa had her husband and her children and the envy and approval of Society, while Augusta did not. None of the suitors who had asked for Augusta's hand in marriage in the ensuing years tempted her to bow to convention and take a husband.

So Augusta had told herself she did not *want* a husband and children. That was for weak-willed females who needed a man to give them social status and a purpose in life.

And she had kept right on telling herself that until now.

Well, Clarissa *was* a ninnyhammer. No one could dispute that. She had not read a book since before Cynthia's birth. Her conversation consisted entirely of parties, pretty gowns, and petty gossip. Once she was widowed, her head was easily turned by the attentions of whichever handsome male fleetingly took her fancy.

The marquess, Augusta had to admit, had been more discreet than most. *He*, at least, though he flirted decorously with Clarissa in public and no doubt made several assignations with her, was decent enough to do nothing that would compromise the widow's reputation in the eyes of Society.

And he had offered to marry her.

Richard, Marquess of Ardath, was an even bigger fraud than Augusta. Everyone in London knew he was a heartless rake, a devil at cards, a hardened bachelor, a crack shot with pistols and a man, in short, who scorned the petticoat rule of home and family.

Any other man would have stayed in seclusion after being jilted and consoled himself with liquor and women of easy virtue, but not he.

He had initiated a search for Clarissa, even though he strongly suspected she had run off with another man. He had taken a personal interest in her children. Now that they were living with Augusta, he called on them every day. And Mrs. Kirby, for all of his protestations that she was *not* eligible for a position as the children's nurse, spent more time these days at Augusta's house than at the marquess's.

Augusta had fooled only herself with her protestations that she was not in love with the marquess. Dorothea's discerning eyes had seen the truth at once, and her friend pitied her. Augusta could have died with the shame of it. The marquess—who could have his choice from among the most beautiful women in London—would hardly settle for a spinster of eight-and-twenty who had not a tenth of her sister's beauty or charm.

The sound of an opening door and a blast of cold air carrying the laughter of children roused Augusta from her grim thoughts.

Richard came into the room first. His coat was saturated with melting snow, and his face was wet and ruddy with cold. There was snow on his black eyebrows, and as it melted it sent a stream of wet into his eyes. He wiped it away with one hand.

"What happened to you?" asked Augusta. "Did you fall into a snowdrift?"

The children came tumbling into the room, giggling. Cynthia's blonde curls were wet, and her nose was cherry red. Gerald and Harry looked as if they had rolled in the snow, and Harry had something held tight in his fisted mitten.

"We had a snowball fight!" cried Gerald.

"How lovely for you," Augusta said, laughing and bending down to help the children out of their wet coats.

"I saved one for you," said Harry. He ran right up to Augusta and threw a small, melting ball of snow directly at her. It hit her collarbone and dropped down the neckline of her new white gown.

Augusta gave a loud shriek that had the butler rushing into the room.

Richard started to assist Augusta in removing the missile from her person, but stopped short in consternation when he realized where it had gone. "Um, are you all right? Do you require . . . assistance of some kind? I could call your maid."

"Thank you, my lord," Augusta said with all the dignity she could muster as she squirmed in embarrassment. She tried to remain still, but the snow was so cold. "I shall go up to my room for a moment, if you will excuse me."

"Harry! What have I told you about throwing snowballs at ladies?" Richard scolded the child when Augusta had left the room. "Gentlemen do not *do* such things!"

"*I* am a lady," Cynthia pointed out. "You did not mind when they threw snowballs at *me*."

"You are a little girl," Richard said, patting her damp curls while she preened and turned her round cheek into his hand. "And you threw quite as many snowballs as we did. You, moreover, are wearing a warm coat and your aunt is wearing only a thin gown."

"Aunt 'Gusta must put on her coat," Gerald said. "*Then* we can throw snowballs at her."

"A delightful notion," Augusta said as she returned to the room in a different gown. This less fashionable one was of green muslin made high up to the throat with practical long sleeves. Richard could tell this was one of her older bluestocking gowns, the ones she wore when she went to sip tea with the other spinster ladies and discuss improving works.

"Are you sure?" Richard asked, surprised.

"Certainly. But I shall warn you that I have quite a good arm for a female and was quite the scourge of our neighborhood after a large snowfall in my salad days."

Eleven

"Ardath!" called one of Richard's most dissolute cronies from across St. James's Street. "Ardath, I say! A word with you, man!"

Richard, who had just paid a visit to his tailor and was in a hurry to call at Augusta's house, stopped in his tracks and blinked.

"Lost in a fog, eh, Richard, old boy?" Justin Linton said jovially. "Surprised you haven't gone off to hibernate as you usually do."

"No. Not this year," Richard said, forcing himself to smile. "Business in town."

"Mrs. Fenshaw's bluestocking sister has you dancing attendance on her, from what I hear," his friend said with a chuckle. "Handsome, dark-eyed girl, if I recollect correctly. One of the fellows saw you in the park with her and her sister's brats. Diddling the sister-mouse while the cat's away, are you?"

"She is a friend," Richard said.

"Oh, no need to cut up stiff. Not one for bluestockings, myself, but I fancy they're grateful enough for the attention to be generous with a man."

"It is not like that," Richard said, realizing for the first time that living in Augusta's pocket could be injurious to her reputation.

"The odds are six to one that you come up to scratch for one of the sisters by the New Year."

"What utter nonsense," Richard said. "Who is saying such things?"

"Just some of the fellows. Having a bit of fun over your being tied to some bluestocking's tether, you know. Just between you and me, old boy, is she worth it? I mean, has she—" His leer told Richard exactly what he was thinking.

"That is none of your business," Richard said crisply.

"Spoken like a gentleman," Justin said. "But you can tell *me.*"

"There is nothing between Miss Oglethorpe and me except friendship."

"You raise my hopes. I wagered you would be shackled to the widow before the New Year. Foolish of her to run off and leave the field to the bluestocking. Jolly good luck for the bluestocking, having a go at catching a marquess."

"The thought never entered her head."

"She is using those children for bait to lure you into her net," Justin said. "It's a pitiful thing to see you so taken in by a bluestocking, of all things. Woman reads *Greek,* of all the queer starts. You haven't been to the club more than twice since you came back to town. We haven't seen you at the tables. Or at Gentleman Jackson's. Or at Angelo's. The woman has you on leading strings."

"That is preposterous. *No one* has me on leading strings," Richard said haughtily. "I make my own decisions."

"Then decide to come along with me now, to the club. The fellows will be glad to see you."

"But I am expected—" He broke off and looked into his friend's face.

He was expected to call at Augusta's house to see the children, but he could hardly say so in the teeth of his protestations that he was his own man.

"That is, I suppose I might put off the engagement until tomorrow. A hand or two of cards would be most agreeable."

"And a bottle of claret or two, as well," Justin said, grinning at him. "To welcome you home."

Richard was hailed as a long-lost brother at White's. The betting books, to his dismay, duly recorded the old odds that he would either marry or seriously compromise Clarissa by the end of the year and the new odds that a certain Greek-reading bluestocking would cast aside her virtue to get her hooks into one of the land's most eligible noblemen by Easter.

He nearly charged into the card room to lay his glove across the bettor's jaw on that one, but forced himself to calm down. Making a spectacle of himself here at the club would be absolutely fatal to Augusta's reputation and his own.

He had laid such bets himself in the past. It would be vastly unsporting of him to cut up stiff now that he was the object of them.

The best way to establish his disinterest in Augusta was to treat the matter lightly.

"A Greek-reading bluestocking," he said, laughing. "Poor Miss Oglethorpe. Although, knowing the woman, she would consider it a compliment."

"An attractive enough woman," Justin suggested.

Richard gave a careless shrug.

"And a worthy one, if one's tastes run to that sort of

thing. Come along now. You are long overdue for a thorough trouncing at cards."

The afternoon passed pleasantly enough, but Richard's conscience pricked as he imagined the children waiting for his arrival. He had looked forward to seeing them as much as he'd anticipated Augusta's usual shy smile of greeting.

Pure mawkish sentimentality, he thought as he took another sip of claret and dealt another hand of cards. Surely the female did not expect him to sit in her pocket all the day long. Under other circumstances, he would have sent 'round a note to explain—er, to *tell* her that he was detained and could not pay a visit to the children today. But he could hardly excuse himself from the men to do so. He would never hear the end of it if he did.

Instead, he went along with the others when they challenged him to a sharpshooting match at Manton's. Even with the best part of a bottle in him, he managed to outshoot them all. Then it was off to Gentleman Jackson's to watch the great man spar with one of his friends.

It was still early that evening when he returned home from a thoroughly satisfying day in the exclusive company of men. He had dined early at the club and pleaded the prior engagement of an assignation with a lady to excuse himself from an evening of revelry at the tables.

Lord, he was tired. He had forgotten how exhausting it was to fritter away one's existence in aimless carousing. It had been a long time since he had drunk himself through the best part of a day, and it had left him feeling slow and stupid instead of all powerful, as it was used to do.

He could hardly call on Augusta and the children in his condition.

He would call on them later this evening, after he had slept off his excesses. He lay down, fully dressed, on his bed. He was asleep before his head hit the pillow.

"It is your fault," Cynthia told Augusta. "You quarreled with him and drove him away."

"I did *not*," Augusta said defensively, and then brought herself up short for explaining herself to a four-year-old. "Lord Ardath obviously had other things to do today."

"But he promised," Cynthia said. "He would not break his promise to us unless *you* made him do it."

Augusta hardened her heart. She was disappointed, too, that Richard had not paid a visit to them as planned. She understood Cynthia's feelings perfectly. But Gerald and Harry were watching the confrontation with wide eyes, and Augusta knew that she could not permit Cynthia to take that tone with her. Not if she expected to establish any sort of discipline at all in her own home.

If Clarissa never returned, she would have the responsibility for rearing these children. She would *not* be ruled by an imperious four-year-old.

She took Cynthia by the arm in a firm grip and marched her right up the steps to her room.

"Owwww! You are *hurting* me!" cried Cynthia.

Augusta curled her lip. She knew very well that she was not. Cynthia had a flair for drama that was going to get her sent to bed without her dinner if she did not stop behaving like a spoiled brat!

The children had disrupted her life, alienated her

from her friends, tortured and caused her cat to run away, drove off her servants, put indelible marks on her furniture, tracked mud on her carpets, and Augusta had borne it all. But there were some behaviors which Augusta must not tolerate if she was to retain her self-respect.

She thrust the child inside the small, formerly neat bedchamber that once was a guest room for Augusta's lady friends when they chose to stay with her. It was virtually unrecognizable now because of the marks on the once-white walls and the toys and papers covered with childish scrawling littered all about it.

"You will stay in this room until you are ready to beg my pardon for your impertinence, missy," Augusta said.

"I hate you!" cried Cynthia when Augusta slammed the door in her disdainful little face.

It hurt. Unexpectedly, it hurt, even though she had received no indication from Cynthia, even when the child was in a *good* mood, that she had the least affection for the aunt who had turned her world upside down in her efforts to be a good surrogate parent to her sister's children.

Before their arrival, Augusta had used to think of herself as a sensible, rational, competent individual. Her household was run efficiently, her clothes were immaculate, her days were filled with interesting books, intelligent friends, and amusing conversation.

I will never be able to live that way again, she thought, and felt the panic rise within her.

Even if Clarissa returned tomorrow, Augusta's old complacency was shattered.

Never again would she view the world from her innate belief in her own superiority. Until now, she had been confident that if she really wished to accept some man's proposal and put the full force of her mind to mothering, she would be extraordinarily good at it, just as she was extraordinarily good at everything else.

After all, even her bird-witted sister Clarissa was a passable mother.

But, put to the test, Augusta found her own performance wanting. She was not good with children, not even when she put her mind to it. Not at all.

The Marquess of Ardath—as disreputable a rake and womanizer as ever lived in London—had continued to concern himself with the children long after he might reasonably have been expected to do so.

Why else, if he did not question Augusta's ability to care for them properly?

That, and because it amused him for a time to do so.

Oh, he was fond of the children. He had quite excelled in the role of affectionate honorary uncle until the novelty had worn off, as she had known from the beginning that it would. If Augusta had led herself to believe that his feelings for herself were at all lasting, the more fool she.

Augusta drew herself up to her full height and squared her shoulders.

Lord Ardath might be able to defuse Cynthia's temper with a kindly word or a gentle look of reproof, but such methods, Augusta had learned, did not work for her.

Show weakness now, and that four-year-old tyrant would be running her household from now on.

Augusta *would* teach that stubborn child and her brothers the proper behavior expected by Society of little ladies and gentlemen, by heaven, or she would die trying!

When she returned to the parlor, she hesitated on the point of having Eliza come to take the boys away so she could be left in peace with her thoughts, but it was not Gerald and Harry's fault their sister was shaping up to be a little shrew.

Indeed, they were as meek as little lambs.

"Is Cynthia being punished?" Gerald asked anxiously.

"Yes," Augusta said defensively. "As she richly deserves."

"Where is Uncle Richard?" Gerald asked.

"I do not know, darling," she said, trying to sound cheerful. "Perhaps he will send a note."

Harry shook his head.

"Uncle Richard ran away, like Mama," Harry said, and went straight to Augusta to bury his face in the skirt of her gown. She patted his head.

"Mama is coming back," Gerald said bravely, but his lower lip trembled. "She promised. She is going to bring us a Christmas surprise."

Harry brightened.

"Yes. I forgot."

Oh, dear.

How in the world was Augusta going to prepare these boys—let alone that little shrew-in-training upstairs—for the likelihood that no such thing was going to happen?

Dinner came and went, but still Cynthia had not come downstairs to apologize for her rude behavior.

Augusta had been on the point of going to her room to check on her, but she hardened her heart.

Cynthia must come to *her.* Augusta would *not* go crawling to the stubborn four-year-old like a suppliant. It would not hurt the child to miss one meal, after all. Augusta and Clarissa had missed enough meals in their rebellious girlhoods when they were being punished, and neither had wasted away in a single night from lack of nourishment.

Augusta spent the evening by the fire, reading a story from Aesop's *Fables* to the boys, who seemed to enjoy it. Their sister's absence did not seem to concern them. In fact, Augusta got the distinct impression that the boys enjoyed the attention they usually did not get when their demanding, precocious sister was present.

Augusta gathered that Cynthia had been frequently punished by her parents by exclusion from the family circle for her imperious behavior and felt somewhat vindicated.

She had arrived at the end of the story, and the boys were trying to cajole her into reading another to forestall Augusta's intention of taking them upstairs to bed, when she heard the door knocker sound.

"It is Uncle Richard," Gerald said eagerly.

Augusta froze in place, staring at the doorway, and Richard walked through it, hat in hand, looking sheepish.

Both boys lunged for him, and Richard picked them up.

"I thought you ran away," Harry said.

"*I* knew you did not," Gerald said smugly.

"Good lad," Richard said. "I am glad to see you still awake. I was afraid you would have been put to bed at this hour."

"As they will be shortly," Augusta said sternly. She was absolutely furious with herself for being so glad to see him. "I cannot permit the children's schedule to be disrupted merely because you have deigned to pay us a visit at whatever hour of the night you happened to find it convenient to do so."

"You are angry with me," he said, sounding contrite, "and you have every reason. I was detained at my club."

"Do not bother to explain," Augusta told him with a creditable assumption of indifference. "Certainly, the way you choose to spend your leisure time is none of *my* affair." It gave her a mean sort of satisfaction to see the way he stiffened up.

"Exactly so," he said with one raised eyebrow. "But I did promise the children, and I am sorry to have disappointed *them*. Where is Cynthia?"

Augusta hesitated, but Gerald stepped right into the breach.

"Cynthia was bad, so Aunt Augusta punished her."

"Was she?" Richard said mildly enough, but it raised Augusta's hackles. "Where is she now?"

"In her room," Augusta said, "which is where she will remain until she apologizes to me for her impertinence."

"Perhaps if I could talk to her—"

"Lord Ardath! I will *not* have you interfere! It will be impossible to instill any sort of discipline in that child if you will persist in letting her go to you to get around me."

"I have no such intention," he said. "Merely, it is obvious to me that you and Cynthia often clash, and I thought I could—"

"You may go to her room if you choose, of course," Augusta said, clenching her jaw.

"Did you lock her in?"

"Of course not," she said, appalled by the thought. "Contrary to what you may believe, I am not a complete ogre."

Richard gave her an involuntary crooked smile.

"So you trusted a four-year-old, on her honor, to stay in her room and be punished until she was ready to apologize," he said. He made it sound extremely foolish.

"But what if the house caught fire? How would she escape from her room?"

He gave a snort of amusement.

"How, indeed?"

"The boys and I will show you the way to her room. It is well past time they were in bed," Augusta said into the anticipated duet of groans.

"Uncle Richard just got here," Gerald protested.

"Perhaps Lord Ardath will be kind enough to call upon us tomorrow, if his social obligations are not too taxing."

"I shall do my best," Richard said dryly.

To Augusta's annoyance, the boys hastened to take Richard's hands as they went up the stairs, even Harry, who used to like *her* best.

She and the boys parted company with Richard on the landing at the top of the stairs, she to put them to bed and he to beard the lioness in her den.

A few moments later, when Augusta had just got Harry into his white cotton nightshirt, a wild-eyed Richard ran into the room.

"Cynthia is gone," he cried. "And I have searched all the upstairs rooms in vain. We must search the rest of the house at once."

Twelve

Augusta regarded the distraught marquess with great exasperation.

Another moment of this, and he would have the boys in tears.

Or wildly rejoicing. Life with Cynthia was not particularly pleasant for either of them.

"The little minx is hiding, no doubt, to throw the household into a pelter," she said. "Do get a grip on yourself, Lord Ardath. That disobedient young lady and I certainly will have words when I find her."

"Yes, I can see for myself how well such methods answer," the marquess replied sardonically.

"I should like to know what you would have done in my place!" she said, with her hands on her hips and prepared for war.

Gerald gave a loud wail and started crying. Harry's face puckered and he threw his chubby arms around Augusta's legs and sobbed.

Augusta dropped to her knees at once to frame Harry's little face with her hands.

"Darling, we will find her. I promise you. Your sister is merely playing one of her tricks on us. You will see."

Gerald tugged on the tail of Richard's coat, and he picked the boy up in his arms.

Plus You'll Save Every Month With
Convenient Home Delivery!

"Do not go away, Uncle Richard," he said tearfully. "Aunt 'Gusta does not mean to be bad."

"I know, Gerald," Richard said, looking Augusta straight in the eye.

Augusta pursed her lips in annoyance. As usual, she was the villain in this piece.

"By all means, then, let us rouse the household and have a big, noisy scene while we beat our breasts and search for Cynthia with our hearts in our throats," she said with a sigh of resignation. "It is precisely what the little wretch wants, after all!"

But after an exhaustive examination of the house failed to reveal the whereabouts of the child, Augusta herself started to panic, especially when a search of the child's possessions revealed that her blue velvet coat was missing.

"She could not have gone outside the house," she said, wringing her hands.

"Not when you trusted her on her honor not to leave her room," Richard said sarcastically, then he held up a hand for peace. "Forgive me, Augusta. That was unjust. I am going to go out looking for her."

She gave him a stiff nod and clamped her lips closed for fear she would say something that would only make the matter worse.

He opened the front door, and Augusta's heart sank when she saw a heavy snowfall in progress.

"I will find her," Richard told Augusta, who could not stop the tears from rolling down her cheeks. "I will bring her back safe to you, I promise."

This was her fault. All of it.

Both the boys fisted their little hands into her skirt, and she put a comforting hand on the shoulder of each.

Richard went straight to his house with the intention of enlisting every able-bodied male servant in his household in the search, only to learn from his butler that Cynthia had arrived under the escort of a person of somewhat dubious appearance a quarter of an hour before his own arrival. One of his footmen, in fact, had been dispatched to Miss Oglethorpe's house to inform the lady that Cynthia was at the marquess's mansion, and Mrs. Kirby had already tucked her into bed.

The person of dubious appearance had insisted upon waiting to speak to the marquess, to the butler's disapproval.

Quite right. The fellow no doubt expected some sort of reward for bringing the child safely to this house, and the grateful marquess was perfectly willing to oblige him.

Richard took a deep breath to steady his racing heart before he joined the man, who had been left waiting in the plain room where his secretary usually saw tradesmen and others whose status deemed them unworthy, in the butler's eyes, of being shown to the book room or one of the parlors.

He beheld a plainly dressed man in a dark suit of inferior cut and fit. His hat was battered, and his shoes were almost worn out.

"Here, my good man," Richard said, smiling graciously as he offered him a twenty-pound banknote. "You have my thanks for bringing Miss Cynthia to my house."

Instead of accepting it with every appearance of gratitude, the man drew himself up stiffly.

"I found her crying and trudging in the snow in the dark," the fellow said. "You should take better care of your daughter, your lordship."

"She is not my—"

"Anything could have happened to her out there. There's a lively trade in selling children, especially those as look like they belong to one of the toffs. She could have been run over in the street by a carriage. Or become ill and—"

"Believe me," Richard snapped, "you cannot suggest a fate for the child that I have not imagined in lurid detail for myself."

He sat down wearily and waved the other man to a chair as well. He badly wanted a glass of brandy, but his hands were shaking so much he did not think he could pour one without spilling it.

"This has been the worst hour of my life," he said

The man narrowed his eyes at him.

"Begging your pardon, your lordship. When you came in so easy and friendly-like, and waving your twenty pounds in my face, I thought, there's a man who does not care. The girl said you were off with your friends and did not care about her at all."

"She is badly mistaken," Richard said grimly. "I am greatly relieved to have her back safely, but I intend to have a stern talk with that young lady in the morning. She frightened her poor aunt and me half to death."

"She said her aunt is mean to her. That is why she ran away."

"What she means," the marquess said, "is her aunt won't let her rule the roost."

The other man nodded.

"Wondered if that wasn't the way of it," he said. "I had best get back to my horses."

"You are a hackney driver?"

"Yes, your lordship," he said.

Richard handed him the twenty-pound banknote, then added a ten.

"For the custom you have missed by bringing the girl here."

The man looked as if he would refuse. Then he gave a self-deprecating smile and accepted it.

Richard took a candlestick and went into the nursery to find Cynthia sleeping fitfully in a small, narrow bed and Mrs. Kirby sitting up in a chair by her side doing needlework by the light of a shaded candle. She stood when Richard came into the room.

"How is she?" he whispered.

"Badly shaken by her ordeal," she whispered back, "but sleeping now. I thought I would sit by her bed for a little while so she would not wake up in the dark and be frightened."

Richard caught the nurse's hand and squeezed it.

"You are so good, Mrs. Kirby. I do not know what we would have done without you."

"Uncle Richard?" called Cynthia.

"I am here, sweetheart," he said, completely abandoning his resolution to speak to her very sternly about her ill judgment in leaving her aunt's house. Her blue eyes were round, and there was still a trace of tears drying on her cheeks.

She scrambled out of the nest of blankets, and he picked her up to cuddle her against his chest. Her chubby arms went about him, and she sobbed against his neck. He could feel the movement when she wiped her running nose on his cravat.

"I am sorry, Uncle Richard," she sobbed. "I will never run away again."

"I hope not. I aged twenty years while you were lost," he said, patting her gently on the back. "Rest now. We will talk in the morning. Good night, sweetheart."

"Are you very angry with me?"

He had to think about it for a moment.

"No." He kissed her on the cheek. "Go to sleep now."

"Good night, Uncle Richard," she said as he sat her down on the bed and Mrs. Kirby tucked her back beneath the covers.

"Good night, sweetheart."

He could have gone to sleep. All the rest of the household was in bed. Or he could have gone out. The fellows were no doubt still at the tables.

He did neither. Instead, he went to his library and poured himself a glass of brandy. His hands finally had stopped shaking.

He had barely lifted it to his lips when he heard the front door knocker sound. He walked out into the hall and opened the door to a distraught Augusta, who nearly fell into his arms, so eager was she to get inside.

"Where is she?" Augusta said, as he steadied her. "Is she safe? Has she taken any sickness from being out in the cold? I know it is improper to call so late, but the boys have only just fallen asleep and I could not leave them until—"

He placed a finger over her lips, because in her agitation she was speaking loudly enough to rouse the household.

"She is perfectly well, Augusta," he said, "and tucked up in bed asleep."

Augusta took a deep breath.

At that moment, Richard's butler came into the hall. He was dressed, but his eyes were only half opened.

Apparently the sound of the knocker had roused him from a sound sleep.

Richard sent him back to bed.

Augusta self-consciously tucked her disheveled hair back into her hat.

"I must see her. I will not wake her, I promise you."

Richard took both her hands in his and squeezed them.

"Of course, my dear. Come along."

He lighted her way up to the nursery. Mrs. Kirby was still sitting beside the bed, but Cynthia was sound asleep. Mrs. Kirby rose and stepped back to give Augusta access.

Augusta approached the bed with her heart in her eyes. She touched Cynthia's soft curls with the most delicate of caresses and stepped back.

"Thank you, Richard," Augusta said when they had left the room and returned to the library. "I know it is silly, but I had to see that she is safe for myself."

"I understand. So did I, when I came home, even though I knew I could trust Mrs. Kirby to take good care of her."

Augusta took a deep, shaky breath.

Richard poured her a glass of brandy, picked it up along with his untasted one, and went to sit beside her on the sofa.

She accepted the glass of brandy, drank it in three fast swallows, and emerged coughing.

"That is *so* good," she said, wheezing for breath. "More, please."

Richard raised his eyebrows, but obeyed.

"I know I am the most inadequate aunt in Creation and she hates me, but I could not bear to lose her," she said, as she accepted the refilled glass from his hand. "And what would I have said to Clarissa if—*when* she came back?"

Richard had begun to lose hope either of them would see Clarissa alive ever again, but he let this pass without comment. He knew that Augusta had the same doubts, but tonight, after such a serious scare, she needed to believe.

"I do not think the child hates you," he said carefully.

Augusta waved this well-meaning thought away.

"Of course she does," she said. "I know nothing about children."

"Neither do I," he said as he rose and took her hand to raise it to his lips, "but I think between the two of us we are managing as well as can be expected."

"They *like* you. Why is it so much easier for men?"

She sounded disgruntled, which was better than having her in despair.

He smiled.

"Because we are superior by nature and by intellect?"

Augusta gave an unladylike snort.

Much better.

"Christmas is next week," she said. "They think Clarissa is going to magically reappear with their wonderful Christmas surprise in tow," she said. "They honestly believe it, Richard. How am I going to deal with their disappointment?"

"How are *we* going to deal with it," he said softly. "I am going to be with you and the children on Christmas, if you will be good enough to invite me."

"I think you are the kindest gentleman who ever lived," she said soulfully. He noted her glass was empty again.

"That is enough for you, I think," he said humorously as he placed the bottle beyond her reach.

She laughed and stood up. She offered her hand. "Thank you for humoring me. I will intrude upon your privacy no longer."

He looked at her proffered hand quizzically for a moment. Then he kissed her on the cheek. With a sigh of surrender, she leaned toward him and laid her head for a moment on his shoulder. He held her close.

"It is all right," he said soothingly when he felt her tremble.

"Forgive me. It is the brandy," she said, drawing back after a moment and smiling bravely. "Shall the boys and I come to fetch Cynthia tomorrow, or will you bring her to us?"

"I will bring her," he said. "I should like to see the boys. Perhaps we might go shopping. The children might like to choose a gift for their mother."

"But she may never—"

He placed his fingertips over her mouth to silence that thought.

"You and I both know that, Augusta. But, if need be, there will be time enough to help the children reconcile themselves to her loss *after* the holiday."

"How did you get to be so wise, my lord?" she asked solemnly. "You certainly exhibited no sign of it before, when you and Clarissa were making an exhibition of yourselves before the eyes of all the *ton.*"

"I had no need of being wise until now," he said.

With that, he walked her out to her carriage in his shirtsleeves and came back into the house, rubbing his arms for warmth.

He considered another glass of brandy, but decided against it.

He was a family man for the short term, it seemed. He would need all his wits about him tomorrow.

Richard regarded Cynthia dispassionately the next day when she stated, categorically, that she would not return to Augusta's house. She wanted to live with him, instead.

She gave him the flirtatious smile so like her mother's and raised her arms to him, certain that this male person, as surely as any of her mother's lovesick flirts, would do her bidding.

Richard realized that Augusta had been right about this child. She *was* a manipulative little hussy who would have all the adults dancing to the tune of her piping if she was given half a chance.

Instead of picking her up as she plainly expected, he said, "What you did in running away from your aunt's house last night was very wrong."

Her smile faded.

"She is mean and she doesn't want me."

"That is untrue. She is your mother's sister, and she loves you very much."

"I do not want to live with her. I want to live with *you*. Mama said that we would all live together. You, Mama, Gerald, Harry, and me. At your house."

"Your place is with your aunt. I am taking you to her now, and you are not to run away again. Do you understand?"

"Yes, Uncle Richard," she said. Her face crumpled. "You do not want me, either."

Bloody hell. Ordinarily he was not one of those men who became unnerved at the sight of feminine tears, but this child was only four years old. Manipulative and selfish, perhaps. But still a child.

He picked her up and hugged her. Her arms clutched his neck convulsively.

"Little one, do you not know that my heart almost

stopped when I realized you were out in the snow, all alone in the dark? *Anything* could have happened to you, and if it had, your aunt and I never would have forgiven ourselves."

"I was *scared,*" she said, sobbing. "It was cold. And it was dark. I want my mama!"

"I know, sweetheart. I know," he said. "But you must stay at your aunt's house now."

Cynthia lifted her tear-stained face.

"Mama is coming back," Cynthia said vehemently. "She has gone to fetch our Christmas surprise, and she will come for us. Soon."

"And when she does," he said, "she will look for you and your brothers at your aunt's house. So let us go there at once."

Cynthia seemed much struck by this argument and donned her coat without complaint.

Thirteen

The absent Clarissa's favorite dressmaker clasped her hands together in anticipation and rushed forward to greet Lord Ardath when he opened the door to her shop. Normally one of her assistants greeted the customers and had them wait, like supplicants, for the *artiste* who would transform them into diamonds of the first water when she had the leisure to see them.

Lord Ardath, however, always received special treatment because he was known to be extremely generous toward any lady who happened to command his fleeting attention, and Mirabelle DuPris greeted him with real enthusiasm.

Her smile froze when he held open the door for three small children and a lady Mirabelle had never seen before. She narrowed her eyes at the woman's clothing, which was perfectly respectable, but hardly in the first stare of fashion. She was a bluestocking! Mirabelle knew the breed quite well, although she had never expected to see one in her shop. She hoped no one would see her leave from it and think Mirabelle had the dressing of her. This could be fatal to her custom.

"Do not touch that!" she cried when the little blonde girl, with the unerring cunning of criminals and small mischievous animals, snatched up Mirabelle's most expensive silk shawl and wrapped it around herself cocoon-style so the tasseled ends trailed to the floor. Mirabelle quickly retrieved the shawl and barely restrained herself from snarling at the child.

Normally people did not bring children into her shop. There was no rule against it, of course, but some things should not have to be stated among civilized persons. A red-haired boy plopped a jeweled turban trimmed with delicate white egret feathers onto his head and grinned. The woman who appeared, amazingly, to be with Lord Ardath, removed the turban from the boy's head and replaced it on the display.

"Please," Mirabelle said prayerfully, wondering what she had done to deserve this catastrophe. Her eyes nearly crossed with the effort to keep an eye on all three children. The youngest had disappeared under a low table and was shaking it so the lovely crystal jewelry beads upon it jumped and rolled. "Lord Ardath, in what way may I serve you today?"

"I need a gift for a lady." He smiled at her, seemingly impervious to her discomfort. How like a man!

"One of those," Cynthia said, pointing to the silk shawl Mirabelle had in her hand.

The youngest child emerged from under the table and took a stunning, three-tiered choker of blue faience beads in the Egyptian style to the woman. The way he gripped the ornament, flinging it about as he walked in a way certain to crack the beads and tangle the silk thread upon which they were strung, made Mirabelle grip her hands together to keep herself from doing something she would regret. All three of these children, she decided, would benefit greatly by having their ears boxed.

"Very pretty, Harry," the woman said, and carefully took the ornament from him. She handed it to Mirabelle, who put it on a high shelf.

"May I suggest a pair of cashmere-lined kid gloves?" Mirabelle said as she signaled a shop assistant to retrieve a box from a shelf. "In white. Or shell pink."

She removed two pairs and held them up—well out of the reach of the red-haired boy who made a lunge for them—for Lord Ardath's inspection.

From the corner of her eye she caught a movement and screamed in horror, "Not the lace dressing gown! My lord, have a pity!"

Just before the smaller boy reached the mannequin with a look of single-minded determination in his eye that quite made Mirabelle's blood run cold, the lady with Lord Ardath reached down, scooped him up, and held him close. She spoke to him in low tones, and he turned around, looked at Mirabelle and Lord Ardath, and laid his head on the woman's shoulder to suck his thumb.

Mirabelle breathed a sigh of relief, only to give a shriek of horror when the little girl triumphantly held aloft a pair of ice-blue cashmere-lined gloves embroidered with seed pearls in a floral design about the wrist. The backs of the fingers were embroidered with silver thread. It was quite her most expensive and most delicate pair of gloves.

"These! Mama should have these!" the little girl said, thrusting the gloves at Lord Ardath, who caught them. "She has a gown just this color."

Mirabelle held her breath. If Lord Ardath purchased that pair of gloves, she would be well on her way to having saved enough to retire in some comfort to a warm climate, or to expand her shop.

He turned the lovely gloves in his hands.

"Yes, I remember the gown. Satin with silver embroidery, is it not?"

Mirabelle's ears pricked. He *was* buying a gift for Clarissa Fenshaw, for she, herself, had created the gown he spoke of. Mirabelle recalled, now, that the lady had mentioned her three children in passing. That affair was still alive, apparently, unless it was a parting gift.

She considered the woman with him.

No. He would not buy an expensive parting gift for a former love with the woman's children in tow. The woman with him now must be a relative. Or a governess, although her manner was not that of a servant.

At that moment, as the marquess thoughtfully regarded the gloves and, Mirabelle could have sworn, had made the slightest twitch of a movement toward his breast pocket, a crash sounded, and a display of artfully arranged embroidered handkerchiefs toppled over to fling the pretty squares of fine linen onto the floor, which was slightly dampened by the dirty pools of melting snow left by the children's feet.

The woman, looking harried, scooped up the red-haired boy so his arms and legs were writhing like those of a captured lizard. Mirabelle regarded the child with utter distaste.

"We must leave this place," Lord Ardath's female companion said through gritted teeth. "Now."

Lord Ardath blinked as if he had been awakened from a deep sleep and looked at Mirabelle quickly enough to catch the poisonous look of hatred she was directing at the children. His penetrating look did not miss the way the children were regarding Mirabelle with small, anxious frowns on their faces and shrinking back against the woman as if they feared Mirabelle might strike them.

Heaven knew her hands clenched and unclenched to prevent her from laying hands on them and tossing them bodily out of the shop.

His lordship removed a banknote from his breast pocket.

The gloves, Mirabelle thought to herself with glee. Never mind that the handkerchiefs were ruined. If she made this sale . . .

"For the handkerchiefs," he said as he handed her the ten-pound note. "Come children. We must not take up any more of Miss DuPris's valuable time."

It was a testament to the gentleman's familiarity with ladies' apparel that he had estimated the worth of the handkerchiefs so accurately. Mirabelle wanted to weep. The look of disapproval in the marquess's eye told Mirabelle that she would not be enjoying his generous custom in the future.

"The gloves, my lord," she reminded him in a desperate effort to salvage something from this disaster. "The little girl seemed quite taken with them. How delightful it is to see one so young with such excellent taste."

She bared her teeth in a smile and reached out to pat the child's head in the hope that this would ingratiate her with the marquess, but the little girl narrowed her eyes at her in disdain.

The marquess regarded her with a polite, distant smile that did not reach his dark eyes.

"I think not," he said. "Come children." He looked Mirabelle straight in the eye. "There are other shops."

"My lord, I beg of you," Mirabelle pleaded.

"Good day, Miss DuPris," he said with a finality in his voice that echoed like a death knell in her ears.

"Well," said Augusta with a sigh as she and Richard herded the children down the street, "that was pleasant. Children, I strictly forbade you to touch anything, did I not?"

"We did not get the blue gloves," Cynthia said, tugging on Richard's coat.

"That shopkeeper stared at the children as if they were monkeys escaped from the zoo," Richard said to Augusta. "She can keep her gloves." He smiled at Cynthia. "We will find your mother something much better at one of the other shops." He glanced at the store window before him. "I have not seen this one before. It must be new."

"You would know, apparently," said Augusta archly.

When they went inside, they found the owner putting merchandise out on a shelf. She was quite a young woman, newly established in business, it was apparent, by the lack of customers and assistants. She was all alone.

She smiled at them when they entered the shop.

"Welcome," she said, smiling at them all. "May I help you find something in particular?"

It was apparent that, seemingly alone among the procurers of feminine adornment in London, this shopkeeper had no idea who the Marquess of Ardath was.

"We want a gift for my mama," said Gerald.

"Something beautiful," said Cynthia. She trotted over to a polished table with folded ladies' shawls on it. Before she could reach for one, the shopkeeper thrust herself before her.

Lord Ardath stiffened.

"Let me see your hands, my dear," the shopkeeper said, smiling.

Surprised, Cynthia held them up for her inspection.

"Lovely. You must have only the cleanest hands if you are to handle the silk shawls. I can see you are a lady of great discernment."

Cynthia preened, although Augusta was willing to bet that Cynthia had not the faintest idea what "discernment" meant.

The shopkeeper held up a ravishing scarlet shawl embroidered with gold thread.

"Now, this would be lovely on your mother," she said, beaming at Augusta. "There is nothing like a bit of color to brighten up the gloom of winter. It takes a woman with dramatic coloring to carry off such a vibrant shade of—"

"Um, I am not—that is to say . . ." Augusta began.

"*She* is not my mother," Cynthia said. "My mother is *beautiful*. The most beautiful lady in the world."

Augusta's hackles instantly rose, but she realized at once there had been no malice in the remark. Cynthia's eyes were innocent. She had simply spoken the truth as she saw it.

"Indeed, she is," Augusta said, forcing herself to smile. "My sister is the children's mother, and quite beautiful. She has dark hair, like mine, but blue eyes, like Cynthia's."

"Oh, I see," the shopkeeper said, apparently impervious to the tension between Augusta and Cynthia. "Then she must be *quite* beautiful."

"But the shawl would look very well on your mother," Augusta told Cynthia.

Gerald made a grab for a crystal necklace dangling from a metal ornamental tree on another table.

The shopkeeper, so quickly that her hands were a blur, touched Gerald's shoulder to distract him.

"I have biscuits in my back room for very special customers," she said to him. "Perhaps you and the other children would like to come with me to arrange some of them on a plate while your aunt and uncle look around the shop at their leisure. Then I will make some tea."

"Biscuits!" said Gerald in glee.

"I knew," the shopkeeper said as she herded the children to the back room, "that you were just the sort of young man who would appreciate a well-made biscuit."

Her brow furrowed, Augusta started to follow. Richard caught her arm to prevent her from doing so.

"But, Richard. Heaven knows what kind of mischief they can get into without us to keep an eye on them."

"She has a way with children," he said. "They will be literally eating out of her hand. Meanwhile, let us have a look around. All the children must have a vote in choosing Clarissa's gift, but it would be a good thing to narrow down the choices, do you not agree?"

"You are probably right," Augusta said with a smile.

"This would suit her," he said, picking up a cashmere bed jacket in celestial blue. Augusta touched the soft, feather-light fabric and noted the intricate seed-pearl embroidery at the neckline and sleeves.

"It seems quite an intimate gift for three children under the age of five to present to their mother," she said archly. Her fingers lingered on the fabric. It was ravishing, but she regarded it with no longing. She had never owned anything so frivolous in her life and would have been at a loss for what to do with it if she had.

"True," the marquess said with a wicked light in his eyes.

"I suppose," Augusta said, "that you have bought hundreds of such garments for various ladies."

"Hundreds," he agreed with a grin. "What a rake you must think me."

"Are you not, then?"

"Well, yes. But I am quite out of practice just now. What do you think of these gloves?"

These were of supple kid the color and softness of butter and lined in cream-colored cashmere. Augusta picked them up with reverent fingers. They were probably the only objects in the shop that she would have chosen for herself, although she suspected they were rather too dear for her purse.

"They are so elegant," she said as she forced herself, regretfully, to put them down. "But rather too plain and practical to appeal to Clarissa. I could see her in this gauze shawl—"

"Look at me! Look at me!" Cynthia said excitedly as she pranced into the room with a glittering crystal and blue velvet bandeau on her head. It was rather too large for Cynthia and listed to one side, but she was grinning from ear to ear. The boys followed. Their faces were liberally sprinkled with biscuit crumbs. The smiling shopkeeper followed. Augusta noted she had a casual hand on each boy's shoulder that would no doubt tighten a bit if either made an attempt to sully the wares with their grubby little hands.

"I had just finished making it before you entered the shop," the shopkeeper said proudly as she regarded the preening little girl with an indulgent eye. "Just the thing for a pretty brunette lady to wear to a ball."

"Mama would look beautiful in it!" Cynthia said.

"That she would," said the marquess, reaching toward his breast pocket.

Cynthia insisted upon carrying the hat box to the carriage, even though it was so large she could not see around it, and Augusta had to guide her with a hand to her back to keep her from bumping into things. Cynthia scowled at the footman who would have taken the box from her.

"Here we are at the carriage," Augusta said. "I will take it now."

"Oh, no!" Cynthia said.

"Then you must step up into the carriage," she said, "and place it on the seat. There you are."

Augusta made as if to get into the carriage herself.

The marquess frowned.

"Surely you are not ready to go home yet," he told her.

"But, of course," she said, blinking. "We have purchased a gift for Clarissa, and thus our errand is discharged. What else is there to do but go home?"

"Unnatural woman," Richard said, shaking his head at her in mock reproof. "I thought all ladies adored shopping."

"And I thought all gentlemen detested it. It seems a perfect waste of time," she said, "when one has nothing in particular for which to shop."

"Such a sensible woman. Are you *certain* you are Clarissa's sister?"

She gave him a little pout.

"My dear Miss Oglethorpe," Richard said for her ears alone. "That look was almost . . . flirtatious."

"It was *not,*" she said, flustered by this observation, which she had to admit—but only to herself—had been somewhat justified. She felt her cheeks grow hot with embarrassment.

"If I were the sort of man who kept a daily journal, I would make a mental notation to record this momentous occasion in it," he whispered. He was so close that she could feel his breath against her ear. He smelled exotically of bay rum.

"Do not be absurd," she said, turning, but their eyes locked over Cynthia's head, and her thoughts skittered away so she could not remember whatever sensible retort she was about to make.

"I want to go to some more shops," Cynthia said hopefully. "Please, Uncle Richard."

Augusta let all her breath out at once and silently blessed Cynthia for breaking the spell before she made a complete fool of herself over Clarissa's marquess.

"Gunter's!" said Gerald.

Augusta had to smile.

She doubted the children had ever set foot in Gunter's before the marquess came into their lives. Now they considered themselves ill-used if they did not have a strawberry Italian ice every second day.

She brought herself up short on the thought that it was not only the children whom Richard had spoiled so completely. Augusta herself had grown quite accustomed to Italian ices for no occasion at all, and, like the children, she would find her old life dreadfully dull when the novelty of squiring a woman and three children wore off for the marquess and he returned to his rakish ways.

Fourteen

London was blessedly thin of company this close to Christmas, when everyone who was anyone had retreated to their country estates for a round of house parties and balls.

Christmas was a mere five days away, and still there was no word of Clarissa.

Richard hired additional Bow Street Runners to search for her. He was hampered by the fact that a very public search would be extremely embarrassing to both himself and to Clarissa if she were discovered to have run off with another man, as he had suspected in the beginning.

He began to fear, however, as Augusta had from the first, that something terrible had happened to her, and she never would be heard from again.

The children, on the other hand, were in a positive frenzy of excitement in anticipation of the holiday. Through it all, they had not lost their faith that Clarissa would come home to them in time for Christmas. Augusta's small house was filled with the mingled fragrances of pine boughs and plum cake and sugar biscuits. She was determined, Richard knew, to give the children whatever joy she might in the likely event that their hopes were to be dashed. And he would do whatever he could to help her.

The children might have to face tragedy all too soon in their young lives.

"Will you have the wedding breakfast here at your house, or at Miss Oglethorpe's?" Richard's Aunt Elvira startled him by asking after Augusta and the children had encountered her one afternoon at the park taking her daily walk, and he had invited all of them to his house for refreshments.

The day had been unseasonably warm for December, and the children had found an outlet for their boundless energy in running circles around each other and around the bare-branched, snow-dusted trees. Tiny puffs of white emitted from their mouths when they shouted to one another.

Augusta had laughed very much that day, and Richard had been struck by the sparkle in her eyes and the poppy red of her cheeks. Harry, having exhausted himself by running after his sister and brother, had come to where Richard and Augusta were seated on a bench, watching the children, and crawled up onto her lap. She smoothed his hair back and kissed him on the cheek. Her eyes had been soft with love.

He reflected that to passersby they would be mistaken for a family, he, Augusta, and the children.

Sometimes when he thought of Clarissa, he could not quite see her face.

"Richard, are you attending?" Aunt Elvira said testily. "Will the wedding breakfast be here or at Miss Oglethorpe's house?"

"Wedding breakfast?" he said, all at sea.

"When the children's mother comes home," she said, "and you marry her."

"We have not decided," he said, appalled by this new scenario.

What if, by some miracle, Clarissa *did* come back with a credible excuse for her absence and she still expected him to marry her? Or what if she were found injured but alive? Only a cad would renege on his promise to marry her under such circumstances.

True, there had been no formal announcement in the newspapers, for his proposal had been quite impetuous. He had expected to marry her out of hand, retreat with his bride to his hunting box for a secluded honeymoon, and thus escape from the inevitable round of insipid prenuptial parties. He had decided he would send an announcement to the press *after* the knot was tied and he and Clarissa were in residence in his town house and ready to receive ceremonial visits from their well-wishers.

If only he had left it at that. But he had seen fit to inform Elvira of his impending marriage, for she had been as close to him as a real aunt during his growing-up years, and, of course, he had informed his solicitor so that all the proper papers could be filled out in connection with the marriage.

He must have been mad.

The last thing on earth he wanted now was to marry Clarissa and embark upon a marriage of uncomplicated lust followed by one of polite indifference and mutual convenience when the passion had cooled.

And Augusta—he could not bear the thought of not seeing her every day. She would be relegated to the status of mere aunt again in the children's lives. Once more she would socialize exclusively with her bluestocking friends, lose herself in her books, get herself a new cat, and erase the memory of these last few weeks from her mind as if they never had existed.

Of course, she would pay the occasional visit to the children. He knew she had become far too attached to them not to do so. But she would avoid meeting him as much as possible. Acting the parts of disinterested brother- and sister-in-law after having grown so close in their mutual concern for the children would be exceedingly awkward.

Impossible.

"Richard!" snapped his aunt.

"I beg your pardon, Aunt Elvira. I was not attending," he said, recalled to his surroundings. Elvira was looking at him quite as if she believed he had lost his mind. Augusta was bent over Gerald, tying his shoelaces, which apparently had come undone. Cynthia, attracted by any talk of parties or finery, had come to lean against Richard's knee. Harry was sitting on the carpet at Augusta's feet, chewing wetly on a hard biscuit.

Elvira gave an unladylike snort.

"So it appears," she said.

"It is customary to have the wedding breakfast at the bride's family home, I know," he said, "but this house is larger, so this might be the more practical choice."

Dash it! The reason he had suggested a simple marriage and a reappearance in town after the fact was to avoid such insipid ordeals as the wedding breakfast and all the attendant tiresome nonsense.

If Clarissa reappeared and he had to marry her, however, there would be no way for him to avoid the more public ceremony. Not if she wished for it.

"Uncle Richard," said Cynthia, frowning. "Why have you not decorated your house for Christmas?"

He blinked at her.

"I had not thought of it. I spend little time here, and—"

"The child makes sense," said his aunt, nodding reminiscently. "When your parents were alive, this house practically glittered with decorations from top to bottom. The late marchioness was a great one for grand entertainments," she said for Augusta's benefit. "There was one endless round of parties here during the whole of the first half of December. Then your parents would retreat to their estate in Scotland and host another whole round of parties there."

"That was a long time ago, Aunt Elvira, and a bachelor household—"

"I remember your mother always had an enormous kissing bough, right there," she said, indicating the chandelier above them. "And entwined red and green satin ribbons that extended from the chandelier to each corner of the room and tied in a bow with trailing ribbons that reached the ground. You cannot imagine anything so delightful."

But Richard could. He remembered it well from his childhood when his parents and brother had been alive. That was precisely why, after his brother's death, he had refused to let the servants decorate the house for Christmas.

And why he had spent every Christmas since alone at his hunting box reading by the fire and taking long, invigorating rides on horseback through the snow-dappled pine forest.

"Your mother's cook had a rare talent for making gingerbread," Aunt Elvira continued. "Each year he constructed a grand house of gingerbread and decorated it with candied fruits and pink sugar icing."

"I remember," he said. At that moment, he could taste the gingerbread on his tongue.

That tradition had ended when he and his brother were old enough to go to school, but the dizzying round of preholiday adult parties in London had gone on until his mother's death when he was at Harrow.

Cynthia's eyes were shining.

"Uncle Richard, can we decorate your house for Christmas this year? Please? Think how surprised Mama will be!"

"Will your cook make a gingerbread house?" Gerald wheedled. "Just a small one. For us?"

Richard could tell from their faces that they had no expectation that he would refuse.

Indeed, he could refuse them nothing. Not when their fate and their mother's was so uncertain.

"Of course," he said. "It is a delightful idea. I shall make the arrangements with the servants."

And if Pierre climbed on his Gallic high horse and declared that making gingerbread was too homely and too English a task to be worthy of his Continental artistry, he could bloody well find himself another employer to exercise his tyranny upon.

"You will join us, of course, Aunt Elvira, to help us decorate the house," he said to his aunt. "Tomorrow afternoon. I shall send a pair of footmen out to, um, bring in the green, although my mother would have found such a country custom quite alien."

"I should be delighted," she said, looking pleasantly surprised. "I shall quite look forward to it."

She stood and offered him her hand. Surprisingly, there were tears in her eyes.

"Welcome back, Richard, my dear," she whispered into his ear when he bent to accept the kiss she obviously intended to place on his cheek. "I have missed my sweet boy so much all these years."

He embraced her warmly.

"Tomorrow, then, my dear aunt," he said. "I will have the carriage brought 'round again."

When he had escorted her outside the room to see her to her carriage, she took his hand as she had done when he was a small boy and leaned confidingly close to him.

"Richard, are you quite certain you are not marrying the wrong sister?" she asked. "Augusta is quite a good sort of girl, and she seems very fond of the children."

"She *is* a very good sort of girl," Richard said, striving for a light tone, even though the thought had occurred to him often enough the past few days, "and of course she is fond of the children—she is their aunt." He squeezed Elvira's thin shoulders. "We both know that aunts are very special."

She laughed and accepted his assistance into the carriage. When she was inside, he kissed his fingertips and pressed them to the glass before her smiling face. She used to do this to him and his brother when they left her house. She waved cheerfully to him as the carriage pulled away.

He turned toward the house to find Augusta standing in the open doorway with a troubled expression on her face.

His smile faded. He knew that look.

"What is it, Augusta?" he asked.

She drew him away from the attentive butler's regard.

"I have left the children alone in your parlor, so we must talk fast and get back in there before they have the room in shambles and all of *your* servants begin giving their notice as well," she said quickly. "Richard, you must not let us put you and your household to such inconvenience if you truly would rather not decorate your house for Christmas."

She cast her eyes down.

"I know Christmas is a difficult time for you, and such trappings of the holiday make you feel melancholy. In general, I believe gentlemen have no taste for such things."

Here was his excuse to extricate himself from his promise, if he chose to take it.

Instead, he smiled to reassure her.

"Nonsense, my dear Augusta. I am quite looking forward to it," he said with perfect truth as he tucked her hand in his arm and escorted her back to the parlor.

Mrs. Kirby, they found, had come into the room and had the children seated quietly at the table, sipping hot chocolate.

Augusta opened her mouth to object that hot chocolate imbibed late in the day seemed to make the children even more excitable and outrageous than usual, but for once she held her peace.

It was Christmastide. They were happy.

She was happy.

Augusta smiled at Richard and took her place at the table, where she buttered a piece of thin, crisp toast for herself and accepted a cup full of the rich, cream-laced chocolate.

He was very different, now, from the dissolute rake she had once thought him. If Clarissa returned, he would make her a faithful husband. And he would be a loving father to Cynthia, Gerald, and Harry.

He was too honorable, she knew now, not to go

through with the proposed marriage if, by some miracle, Clarissa should come back into their lives and want him.

While their uncertain future was hung like the sword of Damocles above their heads, Augusta promised herself that she would enjoy the company of this wonderful man and her sister's children as long as she could.

Fifteen

Richard and Augusta were taking the crisp winter air in Green Park with the children, as had become their afternoon ritual when the weather was fine, when a beautiful young auburn-haired matron dressed in the first stare of fashion excused herself from her party of two other ladies and immediately attached herself to Richard's arm.

"Richard, darling!" she exclaimed, laughing up into his eyes.

"Barbara," he said, giving Augusta a sheepish look. She raised her eyebrows at him and watched with every appearance of rapt interest as the woman walked her fingers up the front of his coat to fasten onto his collar. "I had not known you were in town still."

"Apparently not, since you have not called on me to wish me happy in my marriage," she said, flaunting the enormous diamond ring on her finger. "Darling Giles would be delighted to see you."

"How kind," he said as he detached her greedy little fingers from the collar of his coat and gave her hands a firm, admonitory squeeze. "Behave, Barbara," he added in a lowered tone of voice.

The Honorable Miss Barbara Rafferty—now Lady

Giles Bowland—had been one of his flirts the previous year and had exercised every seductive art in her formidable arsenal to become his marchioness. Failing this, she had latched onto the son of an earl to save face, a match that seemed to agree with her, if her radiant and expensively dressed person was any indication.

"You must know I wish you every happiness, my lady," he said sincerely. Indeed, he had greeted the news of her marriage with heartfelt relief, for he had no wish to hurt her. Giles Bowland, he knew, would make her a much more indulgent husband than he would have done.

"I am so delighted that you have not yet gone into the country," she said, clinging to his arm as soon as he released her hands. "My ball is tomorrow night, and you must not fail me!"

"I beg your pardon?" he asked.

"My ball. My very first ball as hostess. I sent you an invitation. You must have received it. Now that I know you are still in town, I refuse to take no for an answer."

She turned to Augusta, sizing her up with shrewd green eyes. She still had a grip on Richard's arm, and had turned her body to face Augusta's as if she and Richard were a couple and Augusta the outsider.

Neat trick, that.

"I do not believe we have met, Miss . . . ah, now I recognize you, of course! You are dear Mrs. Fenshaw's sister! She and I were quite the bosom bows before my marriage."

Bitter rivals, more like. For him.

"How very interesting," she added, giving Augusta a speculative look. "And these are dear Clarissa's children. How terribly . . . cozy."

"Clarissa had to leave town quite unexpectedly. Felicitations on your marriage, Lady Bowland," Augusta said with a brittle smile. She accepted the white-gloved hand Clarissa's self-proclaimed bosom bow offered her and gave it a firm shake.

"Thank you," Lady Bowland said and returned her attention immediately to Richard. He smiled politely at her companions, but no introduction seemed to be forthcoming. It was like Barbara to forget other women's very existence if there was an attractive man about, and marriage, apparently, had not changed this.

"Lady Bowland is an old friend," he said for Augusta's benefit. The way the woman hung all over him was quite embarrassing.

"Not quite *that* old, my dear Richard," she said insinuatingly. "A pleasure, Miss Oglethorpe. I hope you do not have plans tomorrow evening. I should be delighted to have you come to my ball as well."

"How very kind," Augusta said, "but I would not want to intrude—"

"It would be no intrusion, my dear," her ladyship said with a disarming smile. Her eyes were dancing. "You would be doing me a very great favor, for it would not do to have a half empty ballroom for my first venture as a hostess. Far too many members of our circle have already gone to the country. I am certain Richard would be delighted to serve as your escort."

She gave Richard a coy look that was not entirely devoid of mischief. Richard surmised it was true that newly married women desired nothing more than to inveigle their unattached acquaintances into that happy state. But, knowing Barbara, her motive was more likely a desire to make mischief. It would be her idea of an amusing trick to manipulate events so the notorious rake would have to accompany Clarissa's bluestocking sister to her ball. And if it would cause Clarissa, her old rival, some consternation when the tale came to her ears, all the better.

"Bring her, darling. It will be such fun, I promise you," Barbara said to Richard. She gave an airy little wave of her fingers. "Until tomorrow evening, my dears!" she said in farewell.

Then she joined her companions and walked away, whispering and laughing with them.

Richard glanced at the children, who had been taken to sit on a park bench by Mrs. Kirby while the adults were talking. Augusta's Eliza walked at a discreet distance behind Richard and Augusta like a good little maid for propriety's sake, but Richard was willing to wager the girl had been listening attentively to every word.

"Bosom bow, indeed," Augusta said archly. "You know perfectly well Clarissa could not bear the woman, even though they maintained the polite fiction of undying affection in public with the aim of keeping a close eye on one another's progress with you."

"For my sins, yes," he said, sighing.

"Will you go to the ball, then?"

"Will you?" he asked. "I am doomed to make an appearance. The very least you can do is share my suffering.

"Do I understand," Augusta said, striving for a light tone, "that you are offering your escort?"

"You heard the fair Barbara. She refuses to take no for an answer."

Indeed, the thought of attending the ball with Augusta was not an unpleasant one. Her little maid would accompany them, of course, for propriety's sake. Or, better still, he would enlist Aunt Elvira's services as chaperon. She would be tickled pink to oblige him.

Augusta looked down at her hands. She looked adorably shy.

"It will cause talk."

"There will be talk already. We have quite lived in one another's pockets these past weeks."

"The children—"

"Will be quite content with Mrs. Kirby and your Eliza for one evening. We need not stay long."

"But I have nothing to wear," she said, invoking the most insuperable obstacle of all. "Nothing that would not disgrace us both. In truth, I am not accustomed much to attending balls."

"But, miss!" cried Eliza helpfully as Augusta gave her a quelling look. Augusta had tried to impress upon the girl that she must not speak to her betters in public unless directly spoken to, and she had failed abysmally. "Have you forgotten the new brocade? It would be quite suitable for a ball." She added philosophically, "It is a pity his lordship has already seen it, but that cannot be helped."

"The matter is settled then," Richard said, smiling into Augusta's eyes. "I shall call for you tomorrow evening at, let us say, nine o'clock?"

"Where are you taking us, Uncle Richard?" Cynthia asked sunnily. She and the other children had approached with Mrs. Kirby, but Richard had been so intent upon Augusta that he had not noticed.

"I assume you will be in bed by then, little one, but your aunt and I are going to a ball tomorrow night."

Cynthia frowned.

"But it is *Mama* you are going to marry," she objected. "She will be very cross when she finds out that you have been escorting other ladies to balls."

"Only one ball," he said. "Surely your mother can have no objection to that. Aunt Augusta is her own sister."

Gerald grinned up at Augusta.

"Will you bring us some of those little cakes from the ball? Mama always does so. You can sneak them into your reticule when no one is looking."

"Certainly, my dear," Augusta said as she bent down to give him a quick hug.

Her eyes smiled into Richard's over the child's back, and he found himself unexpectedly delighted by the prospect of escorting her to a Christmas ball that two weeks ago he would have avoided like the plague.

"How beautiful you look, miss," said Eliza in self-congratulatory tones as she placed the finishing touches on Augusta's elaborate coiffure. Because Augusta's hair had been cropped short, Eliza had supplemented it with a small, tasteful demi-wig of false curls she had insisted that they purchase that morning from one of the wigmakers in Conduit Street in order to add height and majesty to the pert style. Then she added the elegant necklet of pearls Augusta's mother had purchased for her upon her come-out, and the delicate matching earrings.

Augusta looked as fresh as she had when she stepped from her perfumed bath, but Eliza looked exhausted. Augusta surmised that it was no easy task to bring a confirmed bluestocking to Eliza's exacting standards. Her old maid would have been prostrate for days after such exertions.

Cynthia and her brothers, forbidden by Eliza to enter and disrupt the proceedings, watched from the doorway to Augusta's dressing room and made many helpful suggestions for Augusta's further embellishment, which Eliza cheerfully ignored.

"Aunt 'Gusta should have a fan," Cynthia said critically.

"Why? So I can fan my flushed face and use it to flirt with all the gentlemen?" Augusta said on a spurt of laughter. "I think not."

"You do not have a vinaigrette, either, do you, miss?" Eliza said pityingly. "I have looked and looked."

"Certainly not," Augusta said scornfully. "What would I do with such a thing?"

"Mama," Cynthia said proudly, "*always* carried her smelling salts."

"I wish I had thought of it when we were at the shops," Eliza said.

Augusta refused to apologize.

"I will have to do without, will I not?" she said cheerfully. She regarded her appearance in the long glass. "You did very well, Eliza, although I do hope the false curls will not fly off during the dancing."

"I anchored them very securely with pins," Eliza said, unsmiling. Although as a rule she was a cheerful, good-natured girl, Eliza took her primary vocation as a priestess in the service of female adornment a bit too seriously for Augusta's taste. "They should withstand anything." She gave Augusta a look full of meaning. "Anything at all. So you needn't be afraid, miss, of . . . enjoying yourself with his lordship to the fullest in any way."

Augusta flushed and looked away, assailed for a moment with a vision of herself and the marquess wrapped in a torrid embrace.

If she had a fan, she could wield it now to good purpose!

At that moment, one of the other maids came to the door and Eliza went to see what she wanted. After a short whispered conversation, she looked back at Augusta with vicarious anticipation in her eyes.

"Lord Ardath awaits," she said grandly.

Richard had just settled himself in a chair by the fire and accepted a glass of brandy from Augusta's butler when the lady herself sailed into the room with three wide-awake youngsters in her wake despite the lateness of the hour.

He stood when she entered the room.

"Uncle Richard!" cried Cynthia as she darted around Augusta and held her arms up to him.

"Hello, sweeting," he said, as he picked her up and gave her a smacking kiss on the cheek.

"When I grow up will you take *me* to a ball?"

"It would be my greatest pleasure," he said sincerely as he tweaked her curls. He set her on the floor as he faced Augusta. He could hardly take his eyes off her as the boys pressed in upon him for their own hugs. "Augusta, you look . . . extraordinary."

"Thank you," she said matter-of-factly. "I shall grow quite insufferable with vanity if all of you do not take care."

"Aunt 'Gusta has false curls on her head," Gerald told Richard. "But do not worry. Eliza has attached them quite securely so they will not fly off when you dance with her."

"Yes," Richard said, straight-faced. "Quite becoming."

"Thank you, my lord," Augusta said on a spurt of laughter as she ruffled Gerald's bright hair. "Now that Gerald has relieved your mind on that score, shall we go before you are privy to any more embarrassing revelations?"

Richard took another sip of the brandy and put it down. Then he offered her his arm to escort her to the carriage.

Before she accepted it, she bent down to give each of the children a hug.

"Remember, my dears. You are to obey Eliza and go to bed without complaint when she tells you to do so."

"Yes, Aunt 'Gusta," they chorused.

Augusta smiled at them and accepted Richard's arm.

"My dear Augusta, this marks an unprecedented event in my life," he said drolly. "I do believe you are the first lady I have ever escorted to a ball who did not keep me waiting a full half hour for her to make her appearance. I had a hot brick tucked into the carriage with Aunt Elvira for fear she would freeze to death while she waited for me to fetch you."

He could not help laughing with amusement when he saw that most of Augusta's staff had managed to find duties that brought them to within sight of their exit from the house and were regarding Augusta and himself with nostalgic smiles on their faces. Clearly, they were delighted to see their bluestocking mistress tricked out in an elegant gown and on her way to a ball on the arm of a presentable gentleman.

"I am not given to such silly tricks, my lord," she said archly as she gave a vulnerable smile of great sweetness to her old retainers.

"I wouldn't have thought you given to wearing false

hair, either," he couldn't resist saying. She gave him a poke on the arm that was a trifle too hard to pass for coquetry.

"Eliza can be quite the little tyrant in her way," Augusta said ruefully. "But the children adore her, so she knows I would never turn her off."

"And you do look very beautiful tonight," he said solemnly.

"Yes," she said without vanity. "Eliza is a treasure. I shall soon have ladies lined up at my door to steal her away from me."

They had arrived at the carriage by then, and Augusta warmly greeted Richard's Aunt Elvira as he helped her inside.

"How glad I am that you are coming with us," Augusta said, squeezing the elder lady's hand. "I shall be happy for someone to talk to, for if I know that Lady Bowland, she will make Richard dance with every woman in the place while I languish at the side of the room."

"Hah! You will not lack for partners, my girl." She squinted at her in the soft glow of the carriage lights. "I always thought you would be quite as pretty as Mrs. Fenshaw if you would exert yourself the least bit. It seems as if your girl knows her work."

"Thank you," she said.

"While we are at the ball, we might bestir ourselves to find a man for you. I have led a full and happy life. I have no complaints. But there is no reason for you to follow my example."

"Matchmaking, Aunt Elvira?" Richard said, displeased by how repellent he found the notion of Augusta marrying another man. "I had not thought it quite in your style."

"Scratch the surface of any female, my dear boy," Aunt Elvira said gaily, "and you will find the heart of a matchmaker beating underneath."

Sixteen

Although there was a light dusting of snow on the ground, the massive oak doors of Lady Bowland's house stood open to the night, and lights shone forth from every window.

Augusta accepted the footman's hand and stepped out of the carriage, shivering with only a shawl to protect her from the winter chill.

As Miss Augusta Oglethorpe, bluestocking and spinster, she was permitted to wear a warm wool coat when she was abroad in the winter. But as Miss Augusta Oglethorpe, fashionably dressed lady on the way to a ball under the escort of a marquess, she must content herself with the very lightest of wraps, for mere comfort must be sacrificed so that she could display her gown and her person to best advantage.

Indeed, she had seen Clarissa go forth into a full snowstorm protected from the elements with no more than a smile and a light silk shawl. On such occasions, her deceptively fragile-looking sister did not even shiver.

Augusta supposed that in time one became accustomed.

When the marquess took Augusta's hand to tuck it

into the crook of his arm, she could not help grasping it with real gratitude.

He looked slightly surprised as he glanced down into her eyes. She was positively clinging to him.

"Shy, Miss Oglethorpe?" he asked.

"Freezing, my lord," she said, trying to keep her teeth from shattering. "I shall be very fortunate if I am not laid on my deathbed with a chill after this night's work."

He laughed at her, but she did not care. His arm was deliciously warm, even though he wore no outer garment over his fine black wool evening clothes.

He smelled wonderfully of slightly snow-dampened wool and bay rum. Every feminine eye turned appreciatively toward him as they entered the house. For a moment Augusta felt . . . proud. From the expressions on the other women's faces, she was the object of a great deal of envy. It was a heady experience.

Augusta drew back when a footman attempted to take her shawl.

"Let him have it, Augusta," Richard said firmly under his breath. His dark eyes were dancing.

Regretfully, she obeyed. For a moment, she envied the elderly Elvira, who wore a long-sleeved dress in gray watered silk under the wool coat she surrendered to the footman.

Then Richard smiled at Augusta and guided her into the ballroom's antechamber with the palm of his hand against the small of her back, and Augusta realized that she wanted to be no one else in the world at this moment save herself.

Upon crossing into the reception room, Augusta's eyes were dazzled by the brilliant light of the crystal chandeliers and the scents of the beeswax candles and the applewood logs burning in the reception room's fireplace. Strings of shiny golden-hued beads intertwined with rich red velvet ribbons were threaded through the chandeliers, and red flowers and green pine boughs decorated the table and fireplace. Hanging above them was a massive kissing bough decorated with tiny white candles, spiced apples and walnuts.

"Lord Ardath," cried their hostess as soon as they reached her in the reception line. "I am so delighted you could come."

Lady Bowland extended her hand to him, and her eyes were avid as they devoured every inch of his person. Augusta glanced uneasily at the lady's husband, who was at her side, but that gentleman seemed to find nothing amiss.

His eyes cooled, though, as he took Richard's hand while his wife was still prattling inanities to him—and would have continued to do so, it appeared, even though her effusions had almost brought the receiving line to an embarrassing halt.

"Lord Ardath," Lord Bowland said stiffly to the man who Society's gossips agreed had been his wife's first choice. "I thought you never came to these affairs."

"Lady Bowland can be quite persuasive," Richard said. "You know my aunt, Miss Steen, of course."

"Miss Steen," said Lord Bowland as he acknowledged Elvira.

"And may I present Miss Oglethorpe. I do not believe you have met. She is Mrs. Fenshaw's sister," the marquess continued smoothly.

Augusta had thought Lord Bowland's light blue eyes quite cold at first, but they warmed and brightened when he took her hand. He was quite handsome when he smiled.

"A very great pleasure, indeed, Miss Oglethorpe," Lord Bowland said, bowing over her hand with such cordiality that Augusta blinked. "I understand Mrs. Fenshaw is gone from London just now."

"Yes. Mrs. Fenshaw's children are staying with Miss Oglethorpe," Richard said.

"Excellent," Lord Bowland said heartily. "So glad you could join us, Miss Oglethorpe. Miss Steen."

The marquess took this hint that they had held up the receiving line long enough and moved on.

"I see that silly little chit Barbara Rafferty still fancies herself in love with you," Elvira said to Richard with a bluntness that surprised even Augusta, who was quite accustomed to Elvira's habit of giving one the branch with no bark on it.

"Nonsense," scoffed the marquess. "She just likes to make mischief. That is why she insisted that I come tonight."

"Why did you, then?" asked Elvira, looking curious.

"I am always eager to accommodate a lady," he said lightly. "Augusta, perhaps you would do me the honor of dancing with me as soon as we settle Aunt Elvira in the card room."

Elvira's eyebrows rose.

"Do you mean to dance tonight, Richard? Without being bullied into it by your hostess?"

"It is what one does at a ball, Aunt Elvira," he said as he showed her into the card room, propped her cane next to her chair, and procured a glass of wine for her from a circulating footman. "Behave yourself, I implore you. Do not leave all the gentlemen with pockets to let. And you must not beg cigars from any of them and smoke in the house."

Augusta's mouth dropped open.

"Oh, yes," Richard said as he put his hand to the small of her back and gently propelled her from the room. "Aunt Elvira is quite fond of the occasional cigar. Has she never scandalized your circle of ladies by setting one alight at one of your gatherings? She enlivened many such in my childhood, once in the company of the royal princes, who occasionally deigned to attend my mother's parties."

"No," Augusta said in disbelief. Her breath was taken quite away by the thought of such rebelliousness against the established order. "She never has. How perfectly splendid of her!"

Richard gave a snort of amusement.

"Bluestockings! I should have known you would find such behavior admirable."

"I want to be exactly like her when I am old," Augusta declared. "It is certainly admirable to set forth to do whatever one wishes in defiance of Society's conventions."

"There are times when you are just like her now," he said. "But not at present, thank the Almighty for small mercies. Let us dance. They are playing the waltz."

"But I do not know how!" she said, taken aback. She had not gone much into company since the dance was introduced at Almack's last year.

"Do not worry. I do," he said, and led her onto the floor. She watched the example of the couples around her with trepidation. "It is only a dance, Augusta. What has happened to that strong-minded lady so determined to do whatever she wishes in defiance of Society's conventions?"

With that, Augusta defiantly placed her hand in his and suppressed a little shiver of excitement when he placed his other hand on her waist. She looked around her for guidance and put her other hand on his arm near his shoulder.

"That is the spirit," he said, laughing down into her eyes. "Now, relax and permit me to guide you."

With that, he nodded in time with the music and swept her into the sea of encircling couples.

"Not dizzy, are you?" he said after a moment.

"No," she said, surprised. "Not at all. It is quite . . . enjoyable."

"Excellent. You are doing splendidly," he said as he drew her closer and began to move faster in time with the music. Dazzled, she looked up at his face, and he winked at her.

She missed a step, and he had to steady her with a tighter grip on her waist.

"You *are* dizzy," he said, sounding contrite. "We may sit down, if you wish."

"No!" she said with a squeak, and clutched him more tightly to prevent him from trying to interrupt the dance.

"Careful," he said, laughing. "If I hold you too closely, the male members of your family are likely to call on me to set an assignation for grass before breakfast."

"Grass before breakfast," she repeated. "Oh! Do you mean a duel? To defend *my* honor? What a ridiculous idea. You need not worry, my lord. There *are* no male members of my family left who might object to your impropriety."

"Then I can compromise you with your good will," he said, chuckling.

"No, of course not," she said frostily as she increased the distance between their bodies. "You know perfectly well I meant nothing of the sort."

"Oh, bother. The bluestocking is back," he said with a sigh. "I knew it was too good to last."

Augusta was flushed by the end of the dance, and she was glad to accompany Richard to the side of the room, where he seated her in one of the gilt chairs surrounding the dance floor and started to seat himself beside her.

"Richard! It was too naughty of you to run off when I had expected to have my first dance with you," said his hostess, who immediately seized his arm. "Everyone knows it is the hostess's duty to dance first with the most distinguished gentleman present."

"That, I believe, would be your father-in-law, the earl," Richard said dryly.

"Nonsense. *He* does not mean to dance tonight! You will excuse me for borrowing your escort, Miss Oglethorpe," Lady Bowland said to Augusta. "I have instructed the musicians to play another waltz."

Richard gave Augusta an apologetic smile and went tamely enough, Augusta thought crossly, to do their hostess's bidding.

She tried not to devour him with her eyes as he and Lady Bowland glided into the sea of dancers as gracefully as a pair of swans.

"Lovely, is she not?" said a male voice close to her ear.

Augusta put a hand to her bosom, not from any coy, feminine impulse, but because she caught her host trying to look down the front of her gown.

"Yes," Augusta said as he seated himself beside her. "Lady Bowland is quite beautiful."

He turned to face her directly.

"Miss Oglethorpe, how do matters stand between you and Lord Ardath?"

"Stand, my lord?" she asked, mystified.

"I am wondering if you and Lord Ardath are lovers."

Augusta stiffened.

"If we were, it hardly would be your concern."

"Oh, you are wrong, my dear. It would make me the happiest man on earth if Lord Ardath would turn his attentions in another direction and leave my wife alone."

"I think it is your wife who has not left Lord Ardath alone," Augusta said. "It was she who came to fetch him for the waltz, after all."

"Let me be blunt—"

"More blunt than you have been already? Please spare my sensibilities, I beg of you."

"I do not believe you have any, Miss Oglethorpe," he said, chuckling. "I am quite a good judge of such matters."

"Possibly so, but this is an excessively personal conversation to have with a gentleman to whom I have only just been introduced."

"Miss Oglethorpe, you are a delight. Will you honor me with the country dance that is to follow this one? I will engage not to step on your toes."

"Very well, but I shall not promise to return the favor, for I am a very indifferent dancer." She could not help noticing the way Lady Bowland smiled coquettishly into the marquess's eyes.

"My dear," said Lord Bowland, "I can see you have

had little experience in these matters. If he glances this way, he must not find you staring at him. Ah. The dance is ended and they are coming this way. Come along now."

To Augusta's surprise, he took her by the hand and led her onto the dance floor. He smiled down into Augusta's eyes when his wife called to him, and pretended not to hear her.

"Ah, this is answering delightfully," the gentleman said with a wicked grin. "The expression on Ardath's face at seeing me walk off with you is priceless. No! Do not look," he added when Augusta started to look over her shoulder. "You must behave as if he doesn't exist."

"But I—"

"How fortunate! Here is a place for just one more couple."

He greeted the other three couples, took Augusta's hand, and, with their linked hands held high, led her to the center of the circle with the other couples when the music began.

"Smile," he told her under his breath. "Try to pretend there is not another man in the world with whom you would rather dance. Let us give my wife and your marquess something to think about, shall we?"

Lady Bowland's eyes narrowed as she watched her husband dance with Clarissa Fenshaw's sister. She was beginning to wish she had not given in to impulse and invited her along with Lord Ardath when she saw them together that day, although it would have been extremely rude not to do so. The wretched bluestocking had looked so dead to fashion in her drab green wool coat with children climbing all over her. Who would have thought she would look so well in evening dress?

"He is just trying to make me jealous," she said, gritting her teeth. "How excessively childish of him."

"*Excessively* childish," agreed the marquess. "So, Barbara, my dear, why don't you tell me why *you* were trying to make *him* jealous by dancing with me?"

Her shoulders slumped.

"That obvious, is it?"

"To me, yes. We knew one another quite well once upon a time."

"Why, Richard? Why did you turn to Clarissa Fenshaw instead of me?"

"Because you wanted to marry a marquess. It did not matter who bore the title. You just wanted to be a marchioness."

"That is not true. I quite fancied myself in love with you."

"Because I am a marquess. I know."

"And Clarissa does not care that you are a marquess, I suppose," she said bitterly.

"Clarissa is just out of mourning and wants to go to parties and put the sorrow of her husband's death behind her," he said. "She makes a very comfortable . . . companion."

"*I* could have made you a comfortable companion," Barbara said with a pretty pout. She caressed the angle of his jaw with her fingertips.

He caught her wrist.

"You, my darling Barbara, would have led me the devil of a dance. Just as you have poor Bowland."

"What utter nonsense," she said with a brittle laugh, but it turned into a little sob at the end.

Richard narrowed his dark, penetrating eyes at her, and she looked down at her hands to prevent him from seeing too much.

"You silly girl," he said slowly. "You married Giles in a fit of pique because I did not come up to scratch, and now you have fallen in love with him."

"Do not be absurd," she said airily.

"Have you considered—forgive me if I am being naive—telling him that you love him?"

"And let him get the upper hand? Do you think I am a fool?"

His silence answered the question for her.

"He married me because I am presentable, I suppose, and his father had been pressuring him to set up his nursery. Richard, he explained it all very carefully to me, that ours was to be a marriage of convenience. I would serve as his hostess and present him with several healthy children, after which I could pursue my own pleasures as long as I was discreet." She gave a scornful laugh. "A perfectly irresistible offer to a lady who had been discarded by a heartless marquess and was eager to save face among the *ton*. How could I refuse?"

"How, indeed?" Lord Ardath said with a sigh.

"I do not know quite how it happened," she said, fighting tears. "Our betrothal and the wedding went beautifully. He was polite and attentive throughout. And our honeymoon—" She had to stop a moment, because her lips were trembling. "It was beyond anything I had imagined. We went to his family's estate in Lancashire in the spring when moors were blooming with bluebells. Richard, I had no idea it could be like that between a man and a woman, at least not among our class. Then we spent the summer at Scarborough. But when we came back to London, he . . . changed."

"You mean you were no longer at the very center of his existence."

She looked up at him, surprised he understood so well.

"Precisely," she said. "I naturally did not want him to think I was going to be a complaisant little wife who would stay home all day to await my lord and master's pleasure, so I immediately set out to establish myself in Society as a married woman by accepting and extending as many invitations as were suitable."

"And flirting with every personable man you encountered while you were in your husband's company," Lord Ardath said dryly.

"Well, of course," she said, deciding he did not understand her as well as she had at first supposed. "I must have my pride, you know."

"And he, in turn, has been flirting with every personable lady *he* encounters."

"Yes, the cad!" Barbara said hotly.

"The cad is going to end the evening with his cork drawn if he does not stop gazing at Miss Oglethorpe's bosom with such fervor."

Barbara jabbed her finger into his shirtfront.

"See here, Richard. If you *dare* abuse my husband—"

"No, I shall leave that to you," he said wryly. "My good girl, can you not perceive the pit into which you have dug yourself with your deception and your tricks?"

"What else was I to do?" she said.

"You might have tried being honest with him. You

could have told him that you wished for a real marriage instead of the customary marriage of convenience."

"And let him hold *that* over my head? It would be *fatal* to let him know how much I care for him," she said. "Once you let a man get the upper hand, you cease to be of value to him."

Lord Ardath cocked his head at her.

"Why do I get the impression you are quoting someone?" he asked pensively.

"Ask any woman. It is common knowledge," she said, tossing her head coquettishly. She lowered her voice and leaned closer to him, for all the world as if they were exchanging an amorous confidence. "He is looking this way." She started to raise a caressing hand to his face, but he raised his own to stop her so their hands were arrested, palm-to-palm, between them.

"You do not learn, do you, my dear?" he said with a sigh.

"I must do *something* to keep his interest!"

"I can suggest several maneuvers that would serve better than this," he said wickedly, "but I hesitate to describe them to a lady in such a public setting for fear of getting my ears boxed."

"Show them to me now," she breathed as she watched her husband from the corner of her eye. "While they are looking this way."

Lord Ardath laughed out loud.

"Behave yourself, you incorrigible brat!"

"You mean for me to act the willing slave for my husband," she scoffed. "To admit to him that I love him, and that all other men are as nothing to me."

"Precisely. If you want any peace, you must get your husband quite alone and without artifice, without guile, tell him the truth."

"You must be all about in your head! Just *tell* him that I love him? That there is no other man in the world for me? That I cannot live without him, and I am going to kill him if he ever so much as *looks* at another woman?"

"And look him straight in the eye when you say it."

"I do not think I can do it," she said, looking agitated. "I would be completely . . . exposed to him. After that, he could do with me what he will."

"It would be most effective, I promise you," the marquess said with a comical leer. "Just be certain that the two of you are quite alone when you embark upon this course of action, or the servants will be quite shocked."

Barbara grew weak in the knees at the mere thought of the scene his words suggested. Giles could be quite exciting and masterful when he . . . she licked her dry lips. But the marquess's advice flew in the face of prevailing wisdom. Her mother, for one—and Barbara always listened to this forceful lady—had told her she must *never* show weakness in the face of the enemy.

"You ask too much, my lord. You ask me to strip myself of my pride."

"Do you want a real marriage with Lord Bowland, Barbara?"

Oh, why pretend? The wretched man could look into her mind and read her emotions as if she had written them in ink on her forehead.

"More than anything," she admitted, "but it is impossible." She put her hands on his shoulders and looked up into his eyes. In spite of her confession, old habits died hard. "Is he looking this way?"

"Miss Oglethorpe is," he said as he caught her wrists to remove them from his person.

"That mouse," she said dismissively. "*She* hardly matters."

"You are wrong," he said, taking her hand and marching purposefully across the room.

"Lord Bowland," said Augusta sweetly, as she slapped his hand away from where it was hovering in the vicinity of her hip, "if you do not stop your hands from roaming, I am going to box your ears."

He threw back his head and laughed.

"You are the most charming flirt," he said.

"Look at me!" she said, exasperated. "I am not flirting. I am serious. Our dance is over. Go away."

"You do not mean it," he said. "You are enjoying our interlude as much as I am." He lowered his voice. "Here they come. She looks absolutely furious."

"That makes two of us," she said.

"Giles," Lady Bowland barked when she and the marquess had reached them. "Kindly stop drooling all over Miss Oglethorpe's bosom and come with me. I have something very particular to say to you."

With that, she grabbed her husband's arm and towed him away. He had the audacity to look back at Augusta and give her an outrageous wink.

She let out all her breath at once.

"What an odd man," she said to Richard. She narrowed her eyes. "You seemed to be having an animated discussion with his wife."

"During which she declared her undying affection for her husband, but flirted with me shamelessly the whole time because she does not want him to get the upper hand in their marriage, if you please."

"How very strange. The whole time he was flirting so devotedly with me, I had to listen to him wax poetic about his wife's lovely face, beautiful form, and flawless skin. Her smile. Her eyes." She gave an eloquent shudder. "Can you imagine enduring such a marriage?"

"No, I cannot," he said grimly, well aware that he had proposed just such a marriage to Augusta's sister. What an idiot he had been! "They are starting to play another waltz. Do you feel strong enough to take a turn about the room with me, or is your stomach still queasy after having to endure Lord Bowland's tiresome raptures on the subject of his wife's perfections?"

"I should be delighted for some exercise, thank you," she said. "I think I quite have the hang of the thing now."

"Excellent," he said, and put his arm around her waist to lead her into the movement of the dance.

It would cause talk, Richard knew, but he could not resist asking her for another dance later, after they had checked on Aunt Elvira and found her cheerfully fleecing a crowd of elderly gentlemen, including their host's father. The earl had drawn his chair quite close to hers, and was laughing uproariously at all her witticisms. She shooed Richard away when he offered to fetch her a cup of tea. She raised her glass of claret to him in valediction when he left.

Two dances with a lady would elicit no comment. Three dances was a clear signal that his interest had been captured. But town was so thin of company at this season, he told himself, that it hardly signified.

And if a third was permissible, why not a fourth? Richard had no idea whether Augusta knew that their behavior was inviting gossip, and he could not bring himself to enlighten her. Her eyes were shining with enjoyment as they romped through a country dance.

After that, Augusta went into the dining room on Richard's arm to enjoy a sumptuous supper of lobster and pâté de foie gras washed down with the choicest wines. Augusta surreptitiously wrapped three dainty cakes in her clean handkerchief and smuggled them from the table in her reticule. He and Augusta exchanged a droll look when they spotted Elvira seated next to the earl in the place of honor at the front of the room, chatting animatedly to him as she matched him glass for glass of wine.

Everyone agreed the ball was absolutely perfect from beginning to end, a triumph for a fledgling hostess, and Lady Bowland had reason to be proud of her first grand occasion in her new home. London might be thin of company at such a season, but the guests agreed that it had been, after all, a sad crush, for anyone of any importance who was in town stayed to the last dance.

The guests looked in vain for their host and hostess in the dining room to toast them at supper, however, for after Lady Bowland towed her husband away from the ballroom, they never returned. The earl rose to the occasion by genially waving the guests off at the end of the evening. He even kissed Aunt Elvira under the mistletoe a time or two.

"Well, that was fun!" the elder lady declared after the marquess settled her comfortably in his carriage. "Four dances! Do not be surprised if the newspapers are full of it tomorrow," she teased.

Richard was glad for the darkness of the carriage,

for he knew his face had turned a dull red. Elvira had a knack for reducing him to the status of schoolboy.

"I should hope the newspapers have more important matters to discuss," he said repressively.

"Everyone knows I have been on the shelf for years," Augusta said matter-of-factly. "Besides, the newspaper correspondents would hardly find the fact that the Marquess of Ardath and the outré Miss Oglethorpe shared a number of decorous dances of any note after being scandalized by the sight of the earl kissing Miss Steen quite thoroughly under the mistletoe."

"He was always an impetuous boy," Miss Steen said coyly. "We saw quite a bit of one another in our respective youths. Then he married and that was the end of it."

"He is a widower now," Augusta pointed out. "It must be very lonely for him, now that his son is married—"

"Listen to the two of you," Richard said, laughing. "And you have the gall to call yourselves bluestockings."

"Let us have no impertinence from you, young sir," Elvira said as she playfully rapped Richard across the knuckles with her bony hand. "It was a delightful evening, and I thank you for inviting me to come with you."

Richard leaned forward and grasped her hands in his.

"My dear Aunt Elvira," he said earnestly. "I am so happy to have found you again."

"I was never the one who was lost, my sweet boy," she said. She sniffed and hunted for her handkerchief. She blew her nose. "Damned wine," she said cheerfully enough. "Makes one maudlin."

* * *

Three wide-awake children were waiting for them when Augusta and Richard returned from the ball well after midnight.

"I tried to convince them to go to bed, miss, but they would not," Eliza said apologetically.

"That is all right, Eliza," Augusta said. "You may go to bed now. I shall tuck the children in."

Eliza curtsied and left the room.

"Did you remember to bring us the cakes?" asked Gerald hopefully.

"Of course, darling," Augusta said, laughing as she dispensed the treats to the eager children. "But I do believe the cake was contingent upon your being good for Eliza."

"We *were* good," said Harry.

"If you had been good, I believe you would now be in bed," she said.

"Mama always brought me the chocolate ones," Cynthia said as she regarded the white cake decorated with strawberries.

"I brought it because it is the prettiest one, but I will take it back if you do not want it," Augusta said, reaching out for it. "I am certain Gerald and Harry would have no objection to sharing it between them."

"No!" said Cynthia, turning her back to keep Augusta from taking the cake from her. "I want it."

Augusta's smile was smug with satisfaction, and Richard had a nearly overpowering desire to kiss her.

"I must be going," he said, memorizing her with his eyes. He knew it was unlikely that he would ever have the opportunity to escort her to a ball again.

"Thank you, my lord, for a wonderful evening," she

said formally as she stepped forward to offer her hand.

He looked at her for a long moment, wishing he could kiss her. Her luminous eyes told her she wished the same.

Harry ended the moment by stepping between them and holding his arms up to Augusta. She picked him up and hugged him.

"Did you miss me, sweetheart?" she crooned into his ear as she pressed a tender kiss on his cheek.

Oh, to be two years old again and loved so much, Richard thought crossly. That was *his* kiss, blast it, and Harry probably did not appreciate it nearly as much as he would have done.

"Yes, Aunt 'Gusta," he said. Then he reached up and gave her hair a good tug, scattering pins and dislodging the little demi-wig. "Your hair did not fall off!" he said gleefully.

"That is enough, young man," Richard said sternly as he grasped Harry's plump hips and set him on the floor. "Go upstairs with Cynthia and Gerald."

All three children blinked. Cynthia looked as if she might protest, but Gerald and Harry took her hands and ran off to do his lordship's bidding.

"Well," Augusta said, watching them leave the room with a surprised expression on her face. "You must teach me that tone of voice, my lord. They never obey *me* half so well."

He turned her around and led her to the chandelier with the kissing bough suspended from it. Then he took her in his arms and kissed her the way he had wanted to do all evening.

They were both breathless when he was finished.

"You are welcome," he said, pleased by the way her

eyes went all unfocused as she gazed dreamily up into his face. He gave her a brief, correct bow and sauntered from the room.

Seventeen

Lord Ardath arrived home only to trip over a huge pile of pine branches heaped on his doorstep. He saved himself from a nasty fall by grasping the railing.

This, he thought, giving it a quizzical look, must be the green that Augusta and the children believed so integral to the celebration of Christmas. There certainly seemed to be enough of it. And there was also a big pile of mistletoe lying next to the pine.

Mistletoe.

He had several times caught Mrs. Kirby and one of the older footmen exchanging significant looks when Augusta's name was mentioned.

It was true that his house had been too long without a mistress. He rarely entertained. No doubt the older servants, who remembered when his sociable parents ruled the household, missed the hustle and bustle of guests who attended the late marchioness's house parties—as well as the vails they left behind.

As his butler relieved him of his hat and coat, he stepped inside the stately house and tried, but failed, to imagine it decked in homely pine branches. He wondered what his long-dead mother would think of the country custom he was about to introduce to her home. He hoped she was not spinning in her grave.

Although his parents always had entertained their aristocratic friends with well-bred ostentation over the holidays, the celebration had little to do with the Christian observance of a holy day. They were, they hoped, staunch members of the Church of England, but they relegated the tradition of the Deity born to a lowly couple in a barn to myth, and they considered the homely, boisterous parties so popular among the lower classes vulgar and unseemly.

Her decorations, though lavish, had no origin in anything that grew in nature.

The thought of three energetic children spreading pine needles through her Mayfair mansion with their sticky little fingers would have given his mother palpitations.

Christmas miracles? An invention of naive souls to give comfort to the credulous. The Marquess and Marchioness of Ardath had not reared their sons to believe in such superstition, yet Richard—the only surviving male of their house—found himself wishing, and even praying, for one.

The marble floors echoed with the clattering of tiny shoes and childish, high-pitched voices lifted in excitement as Harry ran from room to room like an over-exuberant dog begging for attention, Cynthia fashioned a wreath of tinsel and put it on her blonde curls, and Gerald filched so many of the dried apples placed among the decorations for the kissing bough that Richard had to send to the kitchen for more.

Pierre had risen grandly to the occasion, and the scents of cinnamon and hot punch wafted through the house.

"You are doing splendidly, Cynthia," Augusta said when the little girl left off adorning herself and tied a slightly off-center red velvet ribbon to the kissing bough Augusta had been fashioning of wire and pine branches. "I think it needs a bit of sparkle, do you not agree?"

Tiny eyebrows furrowed in concentration, the child carefully placed golden tinsel on the branch. In doing so, she leaned so closely over her aunt's arm that Augusta could smell her sweet, little-girl scent. Her blond curls tickled Augusta's nose, and she could not resist placing a soft kiss on the top of her head.

"Why did you do that?" Cynthia asked, clear-eyed and earnest.

"Because I love you," Augusta whispered.

"Oh," the child said, sounding surprised and rather pleased. Then she scampered away, cat-footed, to chase Harry.

Augusta hastily blinked away a sentimental tear when Richard sat down beside her.

"She is a marvel," he said, enjoying Cynthia's shrieks of laughter.

"I suppose they are getting overheated, and I should—" Augusta said as she started to get up. Richard put out a hand to restrain her.

"Let them be, Augusta," he said, and she sat back down with a slump to her shoulders. "They are doing themselves no harm, and you can see them perfectly well from here."

"They exhaust me," she admitted. "When I close my eyes at night, I cannot sleep for hours as I imagine the horrible things that might happen to them if I am not vigilant. They are so precious. So vulnerable. And they are fearless. Every time I think I have anticipated every danger, they fall into some new mischief that makes my blood run cold. I will *never* be adept at this child-rearing business."

"You are doing extremely well for a lady whose life has been turned upside down and inside out," he said. "Better than anyone could have expected."

She laughed.

"You make it sound almost heroic."

"It is. Very heroic." He took a deep breath. "Augusta, we must talk about the future."

He put his hand over both of hers to still them. She had been fidgeting with the kissing bough because even now, even after almost daily exposure to the marquess's handsome face and figure, she felt a little shiver of restlessness every time he was near her.

"I know," she said with a sigh as she turned her head to look into his eyes, "but not now, if you please. I know someday soon you will want to return to your old life, and the children and I must become accustomed to the idea of doing without you. I always knew this."

"No, Augusta. That is not what I meant. It is about Clarissa."

"Clarissa," she repeated. She leaned forward eagerly. The grimness of his face made her heart plummet. "Has there been news of her?"

"No, my dear," he said, patting her hand. "There has not. I have had runners scouring the city and countryside, retracing every route she could have taken out of London, and they have uncovered not one clue. It is time to call off the search for now and resign ourselves to the idea that we might never recover . . . her."

Her body, he meant. Augusta's mind went numb.

"Augusta," he said, "if Clarissa is dead—"

"Do not say it," Augusta entreated him. "Do not *think* it. She cannot be dead."

"We can cling to that hope. Indeed, I do cling to it. But we must think about how we will tell the children if our hopes are unfounded."

"You are right," she said. "And I have been wrong to deny the possibility. I keep thinking that she has been injured, and one day she will walk into my house and everything will be the same again."

"My dear Augusta," he said, touching her cheek. "How could anything *ever* be the same? Even if she walks through that door tomorrow."

Tomorrow.

And the day after tomorrow was Christmas Eve.

At that moment, the butler entered the room and propped open both parts of the polished mahogany doors. Into the room flowed a sea of neatly dressed bluestockings, some supporting elderly ladies.

"Dorothea! Susan!" cried Augusta, rushing to meet them. She quickly took the arm of the elderly lady scholar and helped her lower herself to a comfortable chair. "What a lovely surprise!"

"Such fun!" Susan said. Her eyes were gleaming. "I have not been to a party to decorate a house for Christmas since I was a child."

Dorothea was less enthusiastic, but she was perfectly amiable when Augusta greeted her. She jumped when Harry walked up to her and took her hand with his sticky little fingers.

"We have hot chocolate," he said, tugging on her hand. He reached his other hand to Susan.

To Augusta's astonishment, her proper friend, who thought all children should be seen and not heard, and, indeed, seen only on rare occasions, tamely allowed herself to be led to a table where a maidservant was placing a tray of dainty cups filled with hot chocolate and topped with cream and cherries. The ladies helped themselves and the children with well-bred little coos of rapture.

"They are rather like cats," Dorothea said pedantically to several ladies as she held a cup so Harry could take a sip. She patted his head as if he were, in truth, a cat. "If they sense your reserve, they will preen for your attention. Discerning creatures, cats. And small boys, too, apparently."

"I found them all, Richard," said Elvira, grinning. "Every bookish lady in London known to Miss Oglethorpe, young or old. The libraries are quite bereft of custom today." At her side was the earl, Lord Bowland's father. He was carrying a huge hothouse poinsettia and a basket of oranges.

"Oranges!" cried Gerald. The earl bent down so the child could select one of the fruits.

"Let us sit down, lad," said the earl, laughing at the boy's enthusiasm, "and I will peel it for you." He ruffled Gerald's red hair. "Bright as new copper, aren't you?" he commented.

"Excellent work, Aunt Elvira. I knew I could depend upon you," Richard said as he kissed the elderly lady on the cheek. "Welcome, ladies. It is a very large house, so we have a great deal of decorating to do before dinner is served."

"You did this . . . for me?" Augusta said, wide-eyed, to Richard.

"Happy Christmas, Augusta," he said, smiling tenderly at her.

He was so wonderful. How would she live without him when he left them to return to his own world?

She pushed the thought away.

There would be time enough to mourn him when he was gone.

"Mama always puts white silk flowers on the kissing bough," said Cynthia, looking at the artificial red roses Augusta had been wiring to the greenery.

"I am sorry, my dear," Augusta said, not taking Cynthia's words for criticism for once. "I am afraid I had forgotten. We always had red flowers on the kissing bough in my parents' house."

Cynthia cocked her head as she considered the arrangement.

"The red flowers are very pretty," she said after a moment. "May I have one for my hair?"

"Certainly, darling," Augusta said.

Cynthia accepted the flower and turned around so Augusta could fasten it in her hair. Augusta improvised a sort of barrette from the wire.

"Here you are," she said. "You look quite pretty."

"Next year, if we ask Uncle Richard, he will buy us white flowers, too," Cynthia said confidently.

Then she turned around, put her little arms around Augusta's neck and kissed her on the cheek. She ran away, light as a butterfly, to chase her brothers.

Augusta sniffed and laughed when a white handkerchief materialized before her blurry eyes.

"I am *such* a watering pot these days," she said.

"I will warn you, it is my last one," the marquess warned her. "Shall I fetch you a cup of hot chocolate?"

"Please. Your boast was not an idle one. Pierre does

make the best hot chocolate in London. It is a pity that it is likely to make the children quite wild."

Later, Augusta and Richard attached greenery and velvet ribbons to the railing of the grand stairway on one side as the earl and Elvira performed the same office on the other. At one point, Richard reached for a bough being held in readiness by a footman and, seeing Augusta was in the way, casually put both arms around her so her back was against his chest.

"Pardon me, Miss Oglethorpe," he said, straight-faced. "This spot seems to have escaped your attention."

She looked over her shoulder at him and found their lips a mere breath apart.

"None of that, boy!" the earl cried gaily. "There are impressionable souls present. We cannot have Miss Steen following your example and taking advantage of the circumstances to throw herself into my arms."

The earl turned to his companion and held out his arms in invitation. Elvira laughed and gave him a coquettish shove that threatened to send him tumbling down the stairs.

"Behave yourself, Frederick!" she said.

"When are you going to erect the kissing boughs?" the earl asked, waggling his eyebrows. "We'll have some prime sport then."

"Later," Richard said, still looking into Augusta's eyes.

By the time Pierre personally served the blazing flambeau of peaches and brandy after a sumptuous dinner of roasted goose, roasted venison, buttered eels, side dishes past counting, and the inevitable pâté de foie gras, the ladies were in a veritable swoon of gastronomic ecstasy.

After the last peach had been consumed, Augusta

looked down the table at Richard, conscious that every eye was upon her.

Good heavens! They considered *her* the hostess!

"I suppose we must withdraw, my dear, so the gentlemen may enjoy their port," Elvira whispered helpfully.

"Oh, yes. Forgive me," she said, rising to her feet.

All the other ladies stood as well, but the earl was having none of it.

"I can look at Ardath's phiz anytime at my club," the old gentleman objected. "And have a drink to his health at the same time." He reached out to pat Cynthia's curls. "I hear a certain young lady has a voice like a nightingale's, and if we are very, very fortunate, she may sing for us tonight."

Richard stood.

"To the music room, then, everyone," he said.

"I hope you have a harp, Lord Ardath," one of the ladies said. "Miss Oglethorpe plays it so divinely. One imagines the heavenly choirs accompanied by such music."

"My mother's harp has been cleaned and tuned for the occasion," Richard said, taking Augusta's elbow to usher her into the room.

"You think of everything, my lord," she whispered.

"I do my poor best," he said modestly.

Eighteen

As long as she lived, Augusta mused, the fragrances of cinnamon and oranges would remind her of Richard.

The Marquess of Ardath, who she once thought the most dastardly of villains, was seated on a chair by the fire peeling an orange while Gerald, Cynthia, and Harry watched him with rapt attention. They looked so precious in their best clothes, the marquess no less than the children themselves.

It was Christmas Eve, the night she had both longed for and dreaded, for once the holiday was over, she must consider a future without him. Yet it was a bittersweet pleasure to pretend, for just this little while, that she was the matriarch of this little family, even though the crushing responsibility of caring for the children was still enough to give a less stout-hearted woman a fit of the vapors.

So must Clarissa have felt as she presided over Christmas Eve celebrations in the past with her husband and children in their home. She began to appreciate anew the heartbreak Clarissa must have felt at losing her husband.

But Richard was *not* Augusta's husband. Clarissa's

children were not truly hers. It was merely an illusion, albeit a pleasant one.

Augusta was wearing a new gown of green satin, one that Eliza had not had to bully her into purchasing. Her maid had brushed her short, dark curls until they were shining and placed a wreath of holly on her head. While she dressed her hair, Eliza remarked sagely that mistletoe would have looked well, but miss wouldn't want to be too obvious. Long carnelian earrings worked with glass beads dangled below her earlobes.

If she was obvious, she did not care.

Good heavens! Had she become one of those women she most despised, those who used artifice and feminine wiles to entrap men into their nets?

Oh, to what depths she had sunk!

Tomorrow could bring happiness or sorrow. Clarissa would come home . . . or not. In either case, Richard would be lost to her.

She had not imagined the way his eyes grew smoky when he had looked at her on the staircase at his house. She had not imagined the ardor with which he had kissed her on the night of the ball.

Yet he had said nothing, nothing at all, about making a life with her and the children once the holiday was over.

It was time they were plain with one another. Tonight, when the children were asleep, she would ask him to state his intentions. She might be pardoned for wanting to look her best when she did so, although the Miss Oglethorpe of old would have scorned such vanity.

He might reject her. But then at least she would *know.*

She would ask him—but not yet. Let her enjoy the

illusion a while longer. After the children were asleep, perhaps, when she and Richard were quite alone.

The thought left her tingling with anticipation.

Perhaps he would kiss her again, like he had the magical night of the ball. Was it too much to ask? One good kiss to savor in her old age?

Who was she fooling?

One of the marquess's kisses would hardly satisfy her for a lifetime. When it was over, she would want another. And another.

"Aunt 'Gusta is standing under the kissing bough!" Gerald shouted gleefully, and ran to kiss her. Harry, not to be outdone, came to kiss her other cheek.

"Thank you both, gentlemen," Augusta said. She felt her cheeks flame with heat at the quizzical way Richard was looking at her. She hastily took the boys' hands and led them back to the sofa.

"*I* have not been kissed under the mistletoe!" said Cynthia mischievously, as she darted to stand under the chandelier with her eyes closed and her lips puckered.

Richard gave Augusta a wry smile and rose to do the imperious child's bidding.

"Later," he whispered to Augusta as he walked over to Cynthia, picked her up in his arms, and gave her a smacking kiss on the cheek.

"Uncle Richard gives *good* kisses," said Cynthia, giggling.

That he does, my girl, Augusta thought enviously.

"Dinner," the butler announced, "is served."

Richard offered his arm to Augusta, but Cynthia rushed around her.

"Me!" she cried. "Take *me* into dinner."

Augusta sighed. She did not intend to spoil her holiday by getting into a row with Cynthia tonight.

She stepped back and chided herself for her disappointment.

"I am afraid not," Richard explained. "The most distinguished gentleman guest present—and that is I—must always escort the lady of the house into dinner."

"Thank you, my lord," said Augusta, pleased and surprised, as she accepted his arm.

For once, Cynthia did not argue, which was, Augusta had to admit, a Christmas miracle in itself. Instead, the little girl accepted with good grace when Gerald rose superbly to the occasion and offered his arm to her with a perfectly executed bow.

In even so short a time, her mischievous but good-hearted red-haired nephew had benefited from the marquess's gentlemanly example. What a wonderful father he would make. As a rule, of course, children rarely dined with the adults of the household. They would be expected to take their meals in the nursery, with their nurse or governess, although in Augusta's small house there *was* no nursery. Nor a nurse. Nor a governess.

Augusta had much to rectify once the holiday was over.

"Is something wrong?" Richard asked.

"I am afraid," she said hastily, "that we have no pâté de foie gras this evening, and my cook—although I would not dare say as much within her hearing—is hardly capable of matching Pierre's artistry with French pastry."

He smiled.

"My dear Augusta," he said, "it is the company, not the food, that brings me to your house. I quite consider myself one of the family."

Augusta felt a silly smile spread over her face, even though the more rational part of her brain told her that it was the sort of pleasantry with which any gentleman might reassure a nervous hostess.

She must not make a fool of herself by reading too much into it.

"Roasted goose!" Gerald cried happily, even though he had dined on this particular fowl often in the past few weeks. If Augusta, as hostess, regretted the absence of the pâté de foie gras, no one else seemed to notice.

What her cook had created was a neat, simple dinner of roasted goose with a modest array of side dishes, but all of them were of the type that would lend themselves to being easily and tidily consumed by young children dressed in their best clothes for the occasion.

Augusta cut Harry's meat in small pieces for him while Richard performed the same office for Gerald. They exchanged companionable smiles over the task. Cynthia deigned to accept Augusta's help with hers. Augusta was flattered that the child did not spurn her help for Richard's.

How far she and Cynthia had come in a few short weeks.

They had just finished dinner and were about to rise from the table when Augusta was surprised by a knocking at the door.

"Mama!" cried Gerald.

Richard put a hand on Gerald's shoulder and looked into Augusta's eyes.

"I am expecting someone," he told her. "He insisted upon delivering his masterpiece in person."

At this, Pierre strode into the room with a huge parcel in his hands. He carelessly swept the china dishes to the side and unwrapped his gift as carefully as if it had been the most delicate of porcelain.

"A gingerbread house!" cried Gerald. Richard caught his shoulder to keep him from diving headfirst into it.

Harry, sly thing, reached out and snatched a candy from it.

"Harry!" cried Cynthia. "It is not Christmas yet. You must not break it before Mama sees it."

Pierre drew himself up superbly.

"But of course, my little Miss Cynthia. This house, it is too grand for now. It is my most exquisite creation, and must follow a Christmas dinner worthy of it."

There was a tradition among simple souls that on Christmas Eve all the animals talk at the stroke of midnight. It was no less miraculous, Augusta thought, that the great Pierre would deign to speak his employer's crude barbarian tongue instead of forcing those present to speak his own more civilized one.

Augusta tried not to feel ashamed because Pierre had swept an expert eye over the broken meats of their dinner and obviously found it sadly lacking.

"But I want gingerbread *now*," said Gerald. His lower lip quivered threateningly.

"Did you think Pierre would tantalize you with this, and leave you unsatisfied?" Pierre said. He snapped his fingers imperiously. "Tonight I give you something even better."

At his signal, one of his kitchen lackeys, dressed in his best clothes, entered the room with a covered plate. Pierre took it with his own hands and dismissed the lackey with a gesture of dismissal worthy of an emperor.

Pierre dramatically drew back the covering cloth to reveal small individual plates containing dainty cut squares of fragrant gingerbread covered with cream, chopped walnuts and candied fruits. At the side of the gingerbread were rounds of spiced apples artfully arranged in the shapes of roses.

Cynthia clapped her hands.

"How pretty!"

Pierre's face softened.

"For you, sweet lady," he said, departing from convention to hand the first plate to the little girl.

Richard's mouth dropped open.

It was astounding enough that Pierre had compromised his artistic vision enough to produce a prosaic English gingerbread. That he would condescend to serve it himself was a favor Richard doubted Pierre would extend to the Prince Regent.

"It is still warm," Augusta said, closing her eyes in rapture when she had taken a bite of the gingerbread. "I have never tasted anything so wonderful in my life."

"But of course," said Pierre, taking this praise as his due.

With that, he bowed grandly to the company, spurned the twenty-pound note Richard surreptitiously tried to place in his hand, and started to leave the room.

Before he could do so, Cynthia jumped down from her chair and ran to clasp him around the knees.

"You cannot go home now, Pierre," she said, looking up earnestly into his eyes. "I am to sing after dinner!"

"Certainly not," he said, conceding to the command of one artist to another. "I will stay."

The marquess had reason later to be glad Pierre had consented to join the family in the music room, even though he knew that after this evening Pierre would be more temperamental than ever.

Richard had arranged for his servants to procure a Yule log from the forest outside London, and when it came time to fetch it, he saw to his dismay that the thing was enormous.

It did not occur to him at first that Pierre would endanger his gifted artist's hands to lend his efforts to help with such a homely task, but the chef gamely grasped one end.

"Did they have to get such a bloody big one?" Richard grumbled under his breath as he smiled reassuringly at Augusta and the children, who had donned their coats and had come outside to watch the men carry in the log.

"But of course, my lord," Pierre said in that superior tone of his. "On Christmas Eve at midnight, one lights the fire and it is to burn through the New Year, or the family will not have good luck."

"*I* will be very lucky if I do not break my bloody back," he said.

"That log is far too heavy for the two of you," said Augusta. "I am going to get some men to help you."

"It must be only men of the family, not servants," said Pierre. It apparently did not occur to him that *he* was a servant, and, indeed, Richard knew he did not consider himself one.

Augusta disappeared into the house and returned with her butler and oldest footman.

"It would not be fitting, miss," said the footman.

"Nonsense. The two of you have been a part of my family all my life," she said. "Now, put your backs into it!"

"Yes, miss," they chorused.

Between the four of them, they managed to wrestle the log inside and set it alight. Strictly speaking, they were not to light it until midnight, but the children would have insisted they be allowed to stay up until then, and Augusta knew they would be hollow-eyed on Christmas Day if she permitted this.

"Remember, Uncle Richard," Cynthia said after she had dutifully kissed him good night. "You are to come here early tomorrow so you will be here when Mama comes for us."

"Yes, my dear," he said solemnly as he exchanged a look with Augusta over Cynthia's golden curls. The children had been talking about their mother's arrival tomorrow as if it were a settled thing.

The simple faith of a child. Too bad it was likely to be crushed.

A smiling Eliza led the children up the stairs to their beds, and at last Augusta and Richard were alone.

"Richard, I—"

"Augusta—"

"Ladies first," he said with a crooked smile.

"No, it is not important," she said. "Or rather, it is *too* important. What were you going to say?"

"I was going to say that the past few weeks have been the happiest of my life, and yet the most confusing."

"Mine, too," she said. "What am I going to do tomorrow when Clarissa does not come for them?"

"I will be here. Early. We will get through this thing together, I promise you." He took her hands in his and chafed them. "My poor girl. Your hands are like ice."

"Only because the fire could not be lit in this room until the Yule log was brought in," she said. "You are so good. I cannot begin to tell you how much your support has meant to me the past few weeks." She drew a deep breath. "Richard, you will most probably think me the most brazen woman on earth, but I must know your intentions."

There. She had said it. Right out loud. She met his eyes square on instead of evading them.

And he laughed.

Actually *laughed!*

"My good girl," he said, "are you *proposing* to me?"

At that moment she wanted to hit him, but he reached out and grabbed her shoulders when she would have turned away.

"My darling Augusta," he said, still laughing. "Pray do not be offended."

"Why should I be offended?" she said waspishly.

"I am not laughing at you, my dear, but at myself," he admitted. "I planned and planned this conversation in my mind. How I would lead up to the moment by easy stages. I would have explained to you that I am getting on in years and it is my duty to my name to set up my nursery. I would have told you how over the past few weeks you and the children had stolen my heart. I would have presented myself as the answer to all your present difficulties in rearing the children alone, for I would be their father in spirit, if not in truth." He smiled ruefully. "I would have promised you pâté de foie gras every day for the rest of your life. I would have been *shameless* in pressing my advantage. And I would have glossed over the fact that less than a month ago I had been willing to enter cold-bloodedly into a marriage of convenience with your sister."

He kissed her hand.

"But you, my magnificent Augusta, have gone straight to the heart of the matter."

"Having done so," she said darkly, "I would be pleased if you would kiss me."

"With pleasure," he said, drawing her under the mistletoe.

"Richard," she said when they had to draw apart to breathe or turn blue. To her embarrassment, she realized that her butler was watching from the doorway with a benign expression on his face. "Yes, what is it?" she said impatiently as she drew herself away from the marquess and self-consciously swept a lock of her hair out of her eyes.

"A visitor," the butler said, still smiling. "One I think you will be pleased to admit."

"Is it—" she began, hardly daring to hope.

Is it Clarissa?

She saw her thought reflected in Richard's eyes as she made an impetuous step toward the doorway.

But instead of her lost sister, she saw one of her footmen standing there with a blanket-wrapped bundle in his arms. With the gesture of a conjurer, he drew back the blanket to reveal a shivering cat with a torn ear and numerous scratches on its skinny frame.

Augusta held out her arms and burst into tears.

"Demosthenes!" she cried.

"Only you," Richard said indulgently, "would name your cat Demosthenes."

"It seemed to fit him. I had never seen so dignified a kitten," she said as she sat by the fire and petted her beloved cat. "You did not know him before, when he was plump and insufferably aristocratic."

"If his present state is any indication, your Demosthenes has proven himself quite a scrapper. Apparently he has decided that tolerating three demonic children is preferable to living without you."

Augusta held Demosthenes up so his back paws were on her skirt, and his face was poised before hers. She gave the cat a quick kiss on the lips.

Richard winced. What an intolerable waste.

"Do not worry, my darling Demosthenes," she crooned to the cat. "I will have you fattened up in no time." She gave Richard a sly look. "I have it on good authority that we are to have pâté de foie gras every day for the rest of our lives."

Richard let out all his breath at once.

She had accepted him on behalf of herself, the children, and, heaven help him, even this cat.

It was the greatest responsibility he would ever accept in his life.

Nineteen

The next morning, all three children rushed into the breakfast room and looked around the room with eager faces.

"Is she here?" Cynthia asked, for all the world as if she expected her mother to be sitting at the table, sipping tea with Augusta.

Then her eyes widened.

"He's come back!" she cried, referring to the cat, which was on the floor at Augusta's feet, dismantling a kipper with relish.

His purring sounded loudly in Augusta's ears, like music after so long without her beloved pet.

"Demosthenes!" cried Gerald.

Demosthenes. The three-year-old still called her Aunt 'Gusta because Augusta was apparently a name so complex his mouth could not get around all its syllables, but Demosthenes flowed off his tongue as if he had spoken Greek all his life. They might take liberties with *her* name, but no one abbreviated the cat's name by so much as a single vowel or consonant.

The cat looked up, saw the children, and leaped into Augusta's lap, kipper and all.

Now her pretty mulberry velvet day gown would

smell of fish, but she hardly cared. She patted Demosthenes's head.

"What *happened* to him?" cried Cynthia. "His hair is all gone."

"Not all gone, darling, and it will grow back. Demosthenes has had many adventures since he left us, but now that he has come back safe to us, we must be very considerate of him."

She gave Harry a stern look, for the two-year-old had reached out for the cat.

"No pulling!" she told him. "You may pet him, very gently, but *not* while he is eating, or he may run away again." She put Demosthenes down on the floor, and the children kept a respectful distance.

"Did Mama come home, too?" asked Gerald, looking, as Cynthia had, as if he had expected to find her in the room.

"It is early yet," Augusta said, feeling guilty for encouraging their hopes. A part of her mourned her sister in her heart, but the rest of her could barely suppress her wonder.

Richard had proposed to her.

He had not precisely gone down on bended knee and poured out eloquent expressions of his undying passion, but he had asked her to marry him so that he might share her burdens and rear her niece and nephews as his own.

Of course, she would have treasured the expressions of undying passion, and could have risen to the occasion with some eloquence of her own, but Augusta had always prided herself on her pragmaticism, and would not reject the man because he did not profess to love her as completely as she had come to love him.

Their wedding, she imagined, would not be the stuff of girlish dreams. He would want a very simple ceremony, Augusta was sure, with the children present, perhaps. And they could hardly go on a honeymoon and leave them to the servants.

They would stay in town. Or perhaps all of them would go on an excursion of some kind. They would marry right away, of course. The sooner they married, the sooner the children would have a stable, secure home.

It would be enough, she told herself.

So why did she feel as if she had been cheated?

She loved the children, she was very sure, as much as any parent could have. More, perhaps, because she had known perfectly respectable persons who neglected their offspring shamefully. But she wanted more in her future husband than a surrogate father for the children.

That was when she realized that she was every bit as foolish as the most naive, brainless maiden who ever wasted her days dreaming of dancing with dukes at Almack's. She had thought herself far too intelligent to be beguiled by such visions.

She even found herself envying poor Clarissa, who, at least, had had his passion.

Augusta remembered the bridal bower Lord Ardath had made of the remote hunting box and shivered with longing.

The roses, the champagne, the intimate dinner for two.

The fragrant bed linens.

She tried to tell herself that Richard did not *love* Clarissa, but that did not seem to matter. Obviously he had anticipated his wedding night with much pleasure.

He would anticipate *their* wedding night, no doubt, with a sense of duty.

And she, who should have more pride, would accept whatever tepid emotion he chose to demonstrate to her.

"When is Uncle Richard coming?" asked Cynthia.

Augusta gave a self-conscious start.

"Soon, my dear," Augusta said. She smiled at the maid when she entered the room with the children's porridge. Because they had become quite spoiled by Pierre's cooking, the porridge had sugar, chopped walnuts, cinnamon, and slivers of apples in it. Because it was Christmas—and because competition with the great Pierre's offerings had put Augusta's cook on her mettle—each bowlful of porridge had a candied cherry on top.

Augusta, herself, was having a poached egg and thin toast. There was also a dish containing another kipper at her elbow, but that was for Demosthenes.

She did not want her breath to stink of fish when the marquess arrived.

The bright winter sun shone in the windows, turning all it touched to gold, and hope was a living presence in the room.

The children were bright-eyed and were tucking happily into the porridge. Demosthenes, her beloved companion, was purring at her feet with the second kipper in his paws.

On such a clear, beautiful morning even she, the bluestocking spinster who had scoffed at daydreams of love eternal, could believe that everything would be all right, even though the fate of her sister was uncertain.

In a way, Augusta had usurped Clarissa's life.

Could she build her future happiness on Clarissa's children and Clarissa's marquess?

Yes, her heart answered. *Yes.*

She was not their mother. And she was not his first choice. But Clarissa could not have loved any of them as much as Augusta did.

She would be so good, so devoted, so unselfish in every way that she would *make* them love her.

Even Richard.

Especially Richard.

"The Marquess of Ardath," intoned the butler, smiling, at the doorway of the breakfast parlor. He had Richard's ivory-headed walking stick in his hand and thumped it on the floor, as if he were announcing a guest at a formal ball.

Amazingly, her staid butler—the same one who had served in Augusta's despotic father's time—had lately developed a sense of humor.

When Richard swept in, preceded by the fresh, invigorating air of a bright winter morning and carrying an armful of sumptuous gifts, Augusta understood the butler's impulse.

He wore a very correct dark blue coat, but there was a sprig of holly in his buttonhole. His dark eyes sparkled. He barely managed to convey his gifts to the table before all three children ran to throw their arms around him and cover his smooth-shaven jaw with baby kisses.

"Let Uncle Richard catch his breath," Augusta said, striving for a light tone, even though *she* would have loved to be the one to greet him with a kiss.

When they married, it would always be like this, she realized. She would always be standing back, unsure of her welcome, hoping for any crumbs that the children may have overlooked.

She was an *awful* person to be thinking such things. They were *children*. Possibly *motherless* children. They needed the reassurance of Richard's affection much more than she did.

Then he smiled at her—a beautiful, intimate smile, just for her—and she saw the light of affection in his eyes.

It would be enough. She would *make* it be enough.

"What did you bring us, Uncle Richard?" Cynthia cried, shoving Gerald, just a little, to get onto Richard's lap first. He patted her blonde curls, but reached over to include Gerald in the circle of his arms. He smiled at Harry and reached toward the table for a small wooden horse to set before the child. The horse had a wide back, just big enough for the plump hindquarters of a two-year-old to rest upon comfortably as he scooted himself about the floor on the horse's wooden wheels.

He did it so naturally, Augusta marveled—patted Cynthia, swept his arm around Gerald so he would not be cheated of attention simply because Cynthia had been clever enough to claim a seat on Richard's lap first, and presented a watching Harry with the first gift so he would not feel slighted.

He was born to be a father. Now, if only *she* could rise to the occasion to become an equally adept mother.

"Thank you, Uncle Richard," Harry said, eyes shining, without being prompted.

Augusta's heart swelled when Harry immediately pulled the horse over to Augusta by its soft leather reins. She lifted him onto the wooden horse's back, and Harry gave a whinny like a horse that caused Demosthenes, pausing for a moment in the important business of eating his kipper, to give Harry a look of lordly disdain.

By then Cynthia was cooing over an extravagantly dressed doll, and Gerald was tossing a ball back and forth to Richard. He had wanted to use the bat as well, but Richard told him he would take him outside later to play with it. "Bats," he said, sounding every bit the benevolent patriarch, "are not to be used in the house."

"Can we play outside now?" asked Gerald.

"Have you finished your breakfast?" Richard asked.

Gerald and the others quickly finished their porridge and held their empty bowls up to Richard for his inspection.

"Get your coats, then," he said as they scurried off. He turned, smiling, to Augusta. "You will join us, I hope?"

"Certainly," she said, feeling self-conscious as his eyes quizzed her.

"You are looking very fine this morning, Miss Oglethorpe," he said. "Another new gown?"

"Yes," she said as she felt her cheeks heat. He knew very well the pretty gown, the carefully arranged hair, the merest touch of rouge on her lips was just for him.

"That Eliza," he said teasingly, "is relentless, is she not? Tell me, is that velvet as soft as it looks?"

He reached for her, but just then three noisy children exploded into the room. Eliza trailed behind them, trying to button their coats on the fly. She had three pairs of mittens in her hands.

She was brought up short at the sight of Augusta, who was no doubt looking daggers at her. Richard's movement had been arrested as he reached for her shoulders.

"Beg pardon, miss, your lordship," said Eliza, looking regretful as she bobbed a curtsy.

"It is quite all right," Richard said kindly, but he gave Augusta a rueful smile. "Come along, then, my dears."

Augusta started to move toward the doorway, where the butler was standing with her coat, but Richard looked down at the table.

"But, my dear Augusta, you have not finished your breakfast," he said. "Do not rush on my account."

"I am not hungry," she said. Not for a lukewarm egg and cold toast.

"Come with us, then," he said, extending one gloved hand to her.

His fingertip had almost touched hers when Cynthia deftly slipped in and claimed Richard's hand for herself.

"It snowed last night," she said happily.

"So I see, my dear," he said, giving Augusta a laughing, apologetic look. "Why do you not go outside with your brothers? You know how they get into mischief with no one to watch them."

"*I* will watch them," Cynthia promised, all puffed up with older sisterly importance. She scurried from the room, and Richard took Augusta's coat from the butler and placed it around her shoulders. She slipped her hands into the sleeves and found herself half in his embrace. But her tiresome butler was watching interestedly from the doorway, so Richard merely buttoned the top button, much as he would have for one of the children, and ushered her outside.

"Harry's lips are turning blue," she observed some time later as the children ran in circles around them, laughing and pelting snowballs at one another. Cynthia, for all her ladylike airs, was quite as noisy and aggressive as either of the boys.

"I can see you are going to be one of those exacting sorts of mothers," Richard said dolefully. "I had wanted to speak to you alone. Do you think they will be tired enough later this afternoon to want to take a nap?"

Augusta gave a spurt of laughter.

"A *nap?* In their overexcited state? On Christmas Day? I hardly think so."

"Oh." He looked nonplussed for a moment. "They do not seem to be paying attention to us now, however. Augusta, about last night."

"Yes," she said, heart sinking at his solemn expression.

Was he about to say he had been carried away by the moment and had reconsidered?

"Mama! Mama! Mama!" cried Cynthia when a hired vehicle pulled up to the door.

Gerald and Harry both started running for the vehicle, and Richard and one of the footmen ran as well, concerned that the eager children might slip and be crushed beneath the carriage wheels.

The person who alighted was not a pretty dark-haired lady but a plainly dressed man unknown to Augusta.

"Your lordship, I went to your house this morning, but the butler said you have come here. I am sorry to disturb you with such tidings on Christmas Day, but—"

"Not here, for God's sake, man!" said Richard sternly as his eyes swept the disappointed faces of the children. "Augusta, please take the children inside." He forced himself to smile for them. He reached out to touch Gerald's bright hair. "We cannot have you coming down with a chill on Christmas Day."

With that, he gestured for the man to get back into the carriage and joined him there.

Clarissa is my *sister,* Augusta wanted to shout.

But she gathered the children and took them inside.

Even Demosthenes seemed to sense something in the air, for he was unusally tolerant of the children. He even allowed the over-affectionate Harry to hold him in his lap for a little while, and forebore to scratch him when his hugging grew too ardent.

Instead, he gracefully slithered out of the boy's hold and leaped lightly to the floor, where he curled up in the small cushioned bed Augusta had brought into the room.

Clarissa. What was happening outside in the carriage?

After an eternity, Richard came back into the house.

He smiled at them, but the smile did not reach his eyes.

"I must leave you for a little while," he said, going to one knee before the children so he could speak to them on their level. "I will be back as soon as I can, I promise." He ruffled the boys' hair and kissed Cynthia's cheek. "Be good to your aunt while I am gone," he said softly, and Augusta's heart sank.

When he left the room, he took Augusta with him. He asked the butler to step inside the parlor and make sure the children were content for a few minutes.

"They think they have found her," he said. His shoulders were slumped. He grasped her hands. "She appears to have lost her memory. She is half wild, Augusta. There are . . . injuries. She has been—" He took a deep swallow. Whatever else he had to say must be terrible. "Have courage, Augusta. If it is she, somehow we will get through this. All of us together."

With that, he kissed her on the forehead and was gone.

Mrs. Kirby arrived a half hour later in one of the marquess's less magnificent vehicles, so Augusta realized that Richard must somehow have managed to send word to his house to dispatch her here to give Augusta her support. Such consideration made her want to weep with gratitude, but she must remain strong and cheerful for the children.

Between them, Augusta, Eliza, and Richard's old nurse valiantly struggled to keep the children distracted, and Augusta thought they had succeeded admirably, but every time a carriage came by the house, the children ran for the window and left little nose smudges on the glass.

"Uncle Richard said he would be back soon," Gerald said. "He will want to be here when Mama comes."

"I am going to sing for her!" Cynthia said, preening.

"I want to show her my horse," Harry said.

"I just want her to come home," said Gerald quietly.

"It is stopping!" Cynthia cried.

Augusta could not restrain herself from running to the window to stand behind Cynthia, not caring that if the carriage contained a social caller, this person would find Miss Oglethorpe gawking out the window like a nosy housemaid.

"It is Aunt Elvira!" said Harry, "and her friend"—which is how the earl had introduced himself to the children.

Bless Elvira for providing this distraction.

She and the earl came bearing gifts—toys and fruit and walnuts and a fat plum cake.

The earl did Cynthia the very great favor of requesting a song from her, and the child, always eager to perform, gladly complied with a pretty Christmas carol Augusta had not heard before.

When she was complimented on her fine voice and the beauty of her song, Cynthia said brightly, "Eliza taught it to me. I have been practicing it so I can sing it for Mama when she comes."

At that moment, the marquess came into the room. Augusta looked up at him. She could hardly breathe. He smiled and shook his head to indicate the woman had not been Clarissa.

Augusta let out all her breath at once. He came to kiss his aunt on the cheek and shake hands with the earl. The children at once demanded his attention, so it was quite a quarter of an hour before he came to sit beside her.

She put her hand over his.

"I am sorry you have been subjected to this ordeal over and over," she said. "I should have been the one to go."

"No, Augusta. We are a family now, or soon will be. It is my responsibility."

They watched Gerald show off his bat and ball to the earl.

"The children have been waiting for her all day," she said.

"I know," he said with a sigh.

Dinner was announced, and Augusta found she was starving. The children fell on the roasted duck with orange sauce like slavering wolves. Their eyes were bright with anticipation.

"Mama will be here soon," said Gerald. "She promised."

The gingerbread house was carried in on a platter by two footmen with all the ceremony reserved for the boar's head, but the children would not touch a crumb.

"Not until Mama arrives," Cynthia said, although her eyes kept going to the little candied fruits she loved so much.

Eight o'clock came and went, but the children were still dressed in their best clothes. There was no thought of putting them to bed.

Instead, Augusta permitted them to stay up and drink hot chocolate with the adults. It was hard to deny them anything when she knew they were destined for such crushing disappointment.

"Augusta," Richard whispered as he took her elbow to usher her from the room while the children played a board game with Elvira and the earl.

When they were alone in the library, he closed the door.

"I think we should marry quickly," he said. "Perhaps at the New Year."

"Yes." The word sounded hollow to her own ears.

She adored this man, but the marriage would be from duty. The children they both loved would always come first.

"When will we tell them?" she asked. "*How* will we tell them?"

Cynthia, at least, was still determined that Richard would marry her mother.

"Not tonight," he said. "It would be too soon."

Too soon after they realized their mother was not coming home.

For if Clarissa did not return to her own children on Christmas Day—and Richard and Augusta had no hope now that she would—she had to be dead.

"Richard, I have no idea how to be a mother," Augusta blurted out. The responsibility was crushing her.

"And I have no idea how to be a father," he said. He kissed her on the cheek. "We will learn together."

He bent forward, and she raised her face to his. But before his lips could touch hers, the approaching sounds of children's voices raised in argument had them breaking apart self-consciously.

Harry pelted into the room with Cynthia and Gerald in hot pursuit. The earl and Elvira followed at a more decorous pace.

"Put it back!" cried Cynthia as she snatched a peppermint stick from Harry's chubby fingers. Augusta recognized it as one that had formed the trim for the gingerbread house.

"Mine!" Harry cried. His lower lip puckered.

In their struggles, the candy stick broke, and Harry managed to snatch it from Cynthia's slackened grasp.

"You bad, selfish boy!" Cynthia screamed. "Now you've spoiled it! We were to save it to show to Mama."

"I *wanted* it," Harry pouted. "Pierre made it for *us!*"

Cynthia burst into tears and Richard held out his arms to receive her. She ran to him and buried her face in his neck when he picked her up and patted her on the back to soothe her.

Of course, she ran right past Augusta to Richard for comfort. She paid no more attention to Augusta than she might pay to a block of wood, and Augusta realized she was jealous not only of Clarissa for attaching this glorious man to her first, but of Richard because Clarissa's children had accepted him so easily.

Then she saw Harry, licking the candy with tears running down his cheeks, and held her arms out to him. He buried his sticky little face in the bosom of her new velvet gown, but she did not care as she cuddled him close.

Twenty

"We really must go," said Elvira. Her eyes were hollow underneath, and the earl had nodded off in his chair twice.

"Mama has not come yet," said Cynthia, who could barely hold her eyes open. Her pink dress was sadly crushed, and the white ribbons in her hair drooped sadly.

Harry was asleep on Augusta's lap. Gerald was walking in slow circles around the floor, occasionally bumping into one of the adults, who would straighten him and let him go on his way, for no one could convince him that he must sit down.

It was ten o'clock, but Cynthia and Gerald would not hear of going to bed. As soon as Augusta tried to rise and carry Harry to his room, he would wake up crossly and plead to stay with the adults.

None of them was willing to say good-bye to Christmas, for when they did, they would have to admit that Clarissa was truly gone.

The earl stood and reached for Elvira's arm.

"We will call on you tomorrow," he said. Then he gave Augusta a sad smile.

When they left, the earl clasped Richard's hand

strongly, as if to give him courage. Elvira kissed both of them with unusual affection.

"My poor dear," she whispered to Augusta when she left.

They all stood in the doorway to wave them off.

The snow was falling, and the full moon illuminated every flake. It was beautiful. Peaceful. On such a night, one could believe that miracles could come true.

"I can catch a snowflake on my tongue," said Cynthia as she darted out the door. The boys followed.

Augusta started out the door after them, but Richard stopped her by putting his arms around her waist and holding her back against his chest.

"Let them go," he whispered. "It will be soon enough for them to face what is to come. We will call them inside before they become chilled."

She relaxed against him and just enjoyed the peace of the moment.

Just then, a coach swept up in front of the house, and the children went running for it. Richard put Augusta aside and they both ran after them.

The door opened, and a tall, distinguished gentleman got out. The children fell back in disappointment.

"My darlings!" cried a familiar, laughing voice. Clarissa's laughter had always been likened to the tinkling of bells. "How glad I am to see you!"

Augusta's mouth dropped open when the distinguished man handed out her sister, who looked so disgustingly radiant and pleased with herself that after her first impulse to burst into tears of relief, Augusta found herself possessed of a strong desire to give Clarissa a hard shake.

Clarissa got to her knees in the wet snow, heedless of

her fine clothes, and held her arms wide so all three children could fall into them and begin talking to her all at once.

"Mama! Mama! Mama! Where have you been?" Cynthia asked.

"We have a gingerbread house, only Harry ate some of it," said Gerald.

"I love you, Mama," said Harry, and threw his arms around Clarissa.

"I love you, too, darling," Clarissa said. Augusta could hear the tears in her voice. Then Clarissa straightened up and looked about, finding Augusta.

"Augusta! What *were* you thinking of to let them play outside in the snow at this hour without their coats on?" She shook her head. "I would have expected you to have more sense."

"You would have expected *me* to have more—" Augusta began, but Richard put a hand on her shoulder to silence her.

"Let us go inside," Richard said.

"Richard? That is, Lord Ardath? Is that *you*?" Clarissa said, squinting in the moonlight. "Good heavens, I never expected . . . Well, this is going to be exceedingly awkward."

As they trooped inside, Richard came face-to-face with Clarissa's escort, who so far had not said a word.

"Lord Ardath," Clarissa said formally, "this is Mr. Ferguson, my husband. Mark, darling, Lord Ardath is—"

"Yes," Mr. Ferguson said with a deprecating smile as he gingerly held out his hand. Richard, looking rather stunned, accepted it. Then he burst into laughter.

"Did I not tell you?" he said to Augusta. "She *did*

run off with another man. Clarissa, if I were not so happy to see you safe, I would wring your neck."

She looked at him as if he had taken leave of his senses.

"Well, I hardly expected you to care very much," she said with a careless shrug. "You never professed to love me. You wanted me to sneak off with you to get married—"

"At St. Paul's? How is it possible to 'sneak off' to be married at St. Paul's?"

"In the *rectory* of St. Paul's. That is hardly the same thing. No parties. No wedding guests. No *cake!* And a honeymoon in your poky little hunting box."

"The hunting box is quite lovely," Augusta said before she could stop herself.

Clarissa's mouth dropped open.

"You took *her* there?" she fumed. "You took my *sister* to your hunting box? How *could* you!" she cried, sounding for all the world like a woman scorned. "You *cad!*"

Richard merely stared at her, mouth agape.

Clarissa's logic—or what passed for logic—had always left him slightly dizzy.

"I went there looking for *you,*" Augusta said indignantly.

"But I *told* you I would be back."

"You also said you were going into the country to *think,*" Augusta scoffed. "As if anyone would believe such a faradiddle!"

"Well, I did," she insisted. Then her eyes lit with affection as she drew Mr. Ferguson forward. "And I met Mark in a country village outside London."

"Impossible!" Richard exclaimed. "I sent Bow Street

Runners to scour London and its environs. No one had seen you."

"Of course not," she said coyly as she looked up at her new husband through her eyelashes. He had the grace to blush. "We wanted to be quite alone. We were married, most romantically, in Scotland and spent a few days at Mr. Ferguson's estate before coming here."

"And marrying at the rectory of St. Paul's is 'sneaking off,' " Richard said bitterly.

"But I *love* Mr. Ferguson," Clarissa said. "He is so kind, so gentle. And he loves children."

"I love children," Richard said softly. He looked hurt.

Clarissa turned away from Richard and smiled down at Cynthia and Gerald, who had been clinging to her skirts all this while. Harry was already asleep in her arms. "Darlings, I must introduce you to your new father. Did I not say I would bring you a delightful surprise? Mark, darling, this is Cynthia, my oldest, and Gerald and Harry."

"You . . . planned this? All of it?" Richard asked, looking and if he had been poleaxed.

"No, of course not," she said airily. "I had planned to bring them a puppy, but a new father is so much nicer, do you not think?"

Richard had no answer for this.

"Clarissa, you selfish little wretch," cried Augusta, indignant on his behalf. "How *could* you be so insensitive?" She stared at Mr. Ferguson until his cheeks grew hot with color. "And where did you meet this man?"

"In a little country church outside London," she said with a rapturous sigh. "I had gone there to think, as I told you. It was so peaceful." She smiled at her husband and squeezed his hand. "And Mark walked in, for his estate is near the church. I recognized him at once, of course."

"You recognized him at once?" Augusta repeated blankly. She looked from Clarissa to Mr. Ferguson.

"He was my first love, when I was fifteen," Clarissa said. "But then we became separated.

"Ferguson," Augusta said, looking hard at the man. "Good heavens! The pastor's son. Our father sent you to boarding school for a year to break off such an unsuitable attachment!"

"I never forgot him," Clarissa said soulfully, "and he never forgot me. He came into his cousin's estate later and left the church, but he never married. It is a miracle."

"A miracle," Augusta repeated. Her eyes met Richard's.

"Mama! Come and hear me sing," said Cynthia, who had been quiet long enough.

"Of course, my darling," Clarissa said.

Cynthia sang the Christmas carol, and no one minded that it was decidedly off-key. Clarissa gave her a hug when she finished.

"I have missed my children so much," she said tearfully to Augusta. "Someday, if you are ever a mother, you will understand."

Augusta was so stunned, she could say nothing in response to this. Richard walked over to her and put his hand on her shoulder.

"Well, we must go," Clarissa said. "Mark has procured rooms for us at the Clarendon. Augusta, may I trouble you to have someone bring the children's coats? I will send for the rest of their things in the morning."

She had conveyed the sleeping Harry from her

shoulder to Mr. Ferguson's, and taken her older children's hands.

Before Augusta could recover from her state of disbelief, the children had been swept away from her and she could hear their excited questions on the wind as she stood in the doorway and watched her sister take them away from her. Richard came to stand behind her and grasped her shoulders. His chin rested on the top of her head.

When she turned to face him, she saw he looked as stunned as she felt.

"I did not even get to kiss them good-bye," she said.

"I know." He led her to the sofa, seated her, then joined her and drew her head against his shoulder.

At that moment, they heard the front door burst open, and three children raced back into the room.

"I forgot to kiss you good night," Cynthia said as she leaped upon Augusta's lap and kissed her soundly on both cheeks.

"Me, too!" cried Harry, clutching her knees.

Gerald hugged Richard. Then, when Cynthia wriggled out of Augusta's arms and into Richard's, he exchanged Richard's lap for hers. After he gave Augusta a sloppy kiss, he jumped to the floor and Augusta picked up Harry to cuddle him for a moment before she passed him on to Richard.

Clarissa stood at the doorway, looking impatient.

"They raised a terrible din until we stopped the carriage," she said. "Now, come along, children. We must go."

"We will come back tomorrow with Mama and Papa to eat the gingerbread house," said Cynthia. She was already calling Mr. Ferguson that.

Gerald took a running leap toward his mother, who

picked him up and exclaimed, "Gerald! You are so much *bigger!* You are not Mama's *little* man anymore."

"Of course he is," Augusta said wistfully as the new family left again without a backward look, once again wrapped up in one another.

That left Augusta and Richard alone.

Augusta looked down at her hands.

"There is no need now for us to marry," she said. "The children are with their mother. We may go back to our old lives."

"Yes, I may go back to brooding at the hunting box whenever Christmas comes around again, and you may go back to reading Aristotle in the original Greek on winter evenings with your cat at your feet." He gave a long sigh. "It seems a rather dull prospect after these few weeks."

Her sigh echoed his as they listened to the clock strike eleven.

He rose and walked to the table, where he fetched a long, flat box tied with red ribbons.

"It is still Christmas, Augusta, and you have not opened your present." He placed it in her lap.

Augusta untied the ribbons and gasped as the tissue inside revealed the expensive leather and cashmere gloves she had so admired in the London shop. He was so sensitive to her that he had noticed her desire for them.

"Oh, Richard! They are so beautiful!"

"Try them on," he said, unsmiling.

She slipped her hand into one and flexed her fingers.

"Perfect," she said.

Still he did not smile.

"Now the other."

Perplexed, she tried on the remaining glove and encountered something solid in one of the fingers. Hands shaking, she removed the tasteful, square-shaped diamond ring from it.

"Richard," she breathed. He placed it on her finger.

"Do you accept me?"

"Now, when there is no need?" she asked.

He swept her into his arms.

"Oh, my dear. There is every need. It took you to save me from myself. I was in danger of becoming a complacent old misanthrope until you and the children stirred up my life."

"The children are gone now. You will have only me."

"My darling Miss Oglethorpe, surely a bluestocking of your stature is intelligent enough to know how one procures more," he said, bending to kiss her.

Twenty-one

The polite world was shocked when the marriage announcement of Miss Augusta Oglethorpe, bluestocking, and Richard, Marquess of Ardath, appeared in the papers on the eve of the New Year.

Publicly, Mrs. Clarissa Ferguson expressed every good wish on the occasion of her sister's surprising marriage, and told everyone who asked about the seemingly mismatched pair that she prided herself upon having brought the lovebirds together.

Privately, she was heard to remark rather pettishly to her intimates that the marquess married her sister in a fit of pique, and she wished her every happiness in her dull honeymoon at his lordship's hunting box.

She was especially annoyed when her children plagued her to take her into hunt country to surprise Aunt Augusta and Uncle Richard for a visit. It seemed they missed them grievously, for it had been several days since the besotted pair had paid a visit to the Ferguson home to take the children for an excursion to the park.

They only desisted after their mother reminded them that Aunt Augusta had entrusted them with Demosthenes, and it would not do to leave him behind.

Many miles away, Lord Ardath, bare to the chest

and his modesty preserved by a sheet pulled to his waist, struggled to one elbow and regarded his wife, who was standing by the window in her white night-gown with her dark curls tousled endearingly about her face. It occurred to him that even after the intimacies of last night, this was the first time he had seen his wife's feet. They were narrow and aristocratic like the rest of her.

"Augusta, my love. What is so fascinating that you have left your husband's bed to admire it?"

"Homer's rosy fingered dawn," she said. "It is miraculous."

He rose, shrugging into his pantaloons with a show of decorum that seemed absurd under the circumstances, and went to stand behind her. He put his hands on her shoulders and kissed the top of her head.

"Truly miraculous," he said, but he wasn't looking at the brilliant pastel light surrounding the rising sun. She turned her face to give him access to her lips.

"Come, my darling," he coaxed her. "The floor is cold."

He swept her into his arms and settled her back on the bed. Instead of joining her, however, he went to the door, had a short, low-voiced conversation with a servant, and returned in a moment with a covered tray, which he settled across her knees.

Eliza entered the room with a teapot and cups, and averted her eyes from the spectacle of her employers in bed while she set the dishes out on a table. There was a smile hovering about the maid's lips when the butler entered with a bottle of champagne and two crystal glasses.

"Thank you," said Augusta, whose face colored

delicately. The servants bowed and were gone, without a word spoken.

With a flourish, Richard removed the cover from the tray across Augusta's knees, and she gave a peal of delighted laughter at the sight of a bowl of hothouse strawberries, a pitcher of cream, and a generous mound of pâté de foie gras with thin toast.

Her laughter did not resemble the dainty tinkle of bells in the least, but the throaty mirth of a woman well satisfied.

How he loved her.

"You remembered your promise," she crowed.

Pâté de foie gras every day for the rest of her life.

"For you, my bride," he said, "and our first day together."